THE FORGED COUPON

&

OTHER STORIES

THE FORGED COUPON
&
OTHER STORIES

LEO TOLSTOY

TARK CLASSIC FICTION
AN IMPRINT OF

MANOR
Rockville, Maryland
2008

ISBN: 978-1-60450-169-8

Published by TARK Classic Fiction
An Imprint of Arc Manor
P. O. Box 10339
Rockville, MD 20849-0339
www.ArcManor.com

Printed in the United States of America/United Kingdom

Contents

INTRODUCTION

IN an age of materialism like our own the phenomenon of spiritual power is as significant and inspiring as it is rare. No longer associated with the "divine right" of kings, it has survived the downfall of feudal and theocratic systems as a mystic personal emanation in place of a coercive weapon of statecraft.

Freed from its ancient shackles of dogma and despotism it eludes analysis. We know not how to gauge its effect on others, nor even upon ourselves. Like the wind, it permeates the atmosphere we breathe, and baffles while it stimulates the mind with its intangible but compelling force.

This psychic power, which the dead weight of materialism is impotent to suppress, is revealed in the lives and writings of men of the most diverse creeds and nationalities. Apart from those who, like Buddha and Mahomet, have been raised to the height of demi-gods by worshipping millions, there are names which leap inevitably to the mind—such names as Savonarola, Luther, Calvin, Rousseau—which stand for types and exemplars of spiritual aspiration. To this high priesthood of the quick among the dead, who can doubt that time will admit Leo Tolstoy—a genius whose greatness has been obscured from us rather than enhanced by his duality; a realist who strove to demolish the mysticism of Christianity, and became himself a mystic in the contemplation of Nature; a man of ardent temperament and robust physique, keenly susceptible to human passions and desires, who battled with himself from early manhood until the spirit, gathering strength with years, inexorably subdued the flesh.

Tolstoy the realist steps without cavil into the front rank of modern writers; Tolstoy the idealist has been constantly derided and scorned by men of like birth and education with himself—his altruism denounced as impracticable, his preaching compared with his mode of life to prove him inconsistent, if not insincere. This is the prevailing attitude of politicians and literary men.

Must one conclude that the mass of mankind has lost touch with idealism? On the contrary, in spite of modern materialism, or even because of it, many leaders of spiritual thought have arisen in our times, and have won the ear of vast audiences. Their message is a call to a simpler life, to a recognition of the responsibilities of wealth, to the avoidance of war by arbitration, and sinking of class hatred in a deep sense of universal brotherhood.

Unhappily, when an idealistic creed is formulated in precise and dogmatic language, it invariably loses something of its pristine beauty in the process of transmutation. Hence the Positivist philosophy of Comte, though embodying noble aspirations, has had but a limited influence. Again, the poetry of Robert Browning, though less frankly altruistic than that of Cowper or Wordsworth, is inherently ethical, and reveals strong sympathy with sinning and suffering humanity, but it is masked by a manner that is sometimes uncouth and frequently obscure. Owing to these, and other instances, idealism suggests to the world at large a vague sentimentality peculiar to the poets, a bloodless abstraction toyed with by philosophers, which must remain a closed book to struggling humanity.

Yet Tolstoy found true idealism in the toiling peasant who believed in God, rather than in his intellectual superior who believed in himself in the first place, and gave a conventional assent to the existence of a deity in the second. For the peasant was still religious at heart with a naive unquestioning faith—more characteristic of the fourteenth or fifteenth century than of to-day—and still fervently aspired to God although sunk in superstition and held down by the despotism of the Greek Church. It was the cumbrous ritual and dogma of the orthodox state religion which roused Tolstoy to impassioned protests, and led him step by step to separate the core of Christianity from its sacerdotal shell, thus bringing upon himself the ban of excommunication.

The signal mark of the reprobation of "Holy Synod" was slow in coming—it did not, in fact, become absolute until a couple of years after the publication of "Resurrection," in 1901, in spite of the attitude of fierce hostility to Church and State which Tolstoy had maintained for so long. This hostility, of which the seeds were primarily sown by the closing of his school and inquisition of his private papers in the summer of 1862, soon grew to proportions far greater than those arising from a personal wrong. The dumb and submissive moujik found in Tolstoy a living voice to express his sufferings.

Tolstoy was well fitted by nature and circumstances to be the peasant's spokesman. He had been brought into intimate contact with him in the varying conditions of peace and war, and he knew him at his worst and best. The old home of the family, Yasnaya Polyana, where Tolstoy, his brothers and sister, spent their early years in charge of two guardian aunts, was not only a halting-place for pilgrims journeying to and from the great monastic shrines, but gave shelter to a number of persons of enfeebled minds belonging to the peasant class, with whom the devout and kindly Aunt Alexandra spent many hours daily in religious conversation and prayer.

In "Childhood" Tolstoy apostrophises with feeling one of those "innocents," a man named Grisha, "whose faith was so strong that you felt the nearness of God, your love so ardent that the words flowed from your lips uncontrolled by your reason. And how did you celebrate his Majesty when, words failing you, you prostrated yourself on the ground, bathed in tears" This picture of humble religious faith was amongst Tolstoy's earliest memories, and it returned to comfort him and uplift his soul when it was tossed and engulfed by seas of doubt. But the affection he felt in boyhood towards the moujiks became tinged with contempt when his attempts to improve their condition—some of which are described in "Anna Karenina" and in the "Landlord's Morning"—ended in failure, owing to the ignorance and obstinacy of the people. It was not till he passed through the ordeal of war in Turkey and the Crimea that he discovered in the common soldier who fought by his side an unconscious heroism, an unquestioning faith in God, a kindliness and simplicity of heart rarely possessed by his commanding officer.

The impressions made upon Tolstoy during this period of active service gave vivid reality to the battle-scenes in "War and Peace," and are traceable in the reflections and conversation of the two heroes, Prince Andre and Pierre Besukhov. On the eve of the battle of Borodino, Prince Andre, talking with Pierre in the presence of his devoted soldier-servant Timokhine, says,—"'Success cannot possibly be, nor has it ever been, the result of strategy or fire-arms or numbers.'"

"'Then what does it result from?' said Pierre.

"'From the feeling that is in me, that is in him'—pointing to Timokhine—'and that is in each individual soldier.'"

He then contrasts the different spirit animating the officers and the men.

"'The former,' he says, 'have nothing in view but their personal interests. The critical moment for them is the moment at which they are able to supplant a rival, to win a cross or a new order. I see only one thing. To-morrow one hundred thousand Russians and one hundred thousand Frenchmen will meet to fight; they who fight the hardest and spare themselves the least will win the day.'

"'There's the truth, your Excellency, the real truth,' murmurs Timokhine; 'it is not a time to spare oneself. Would you believe it, the men of my battalion have not tasted brandy? "It's not a day for that," they said.'"

During the momentous battle which followed, Pierre was struck by the steadfastness under fire which has always distinguished the Russian soldier.

"The fall of each man acted as an increasing stimulus. The faces of the soldiers brightened more and more, as if challenging the storm let loose on them."

In contrast with this picture of fine "morale" is that of the young white-faced officer, looking nervously about him as he walks backwards with lowered sword.

In other places Tolstoy does full justice to the courage and patriotism of all grades in the Russian army, but it is constantly evident that his sympathies are most heartily with the rank and file. What genuine feeling and affection rings in this sketch of Plato, a common soldier, in "War and Peace!"

"Plato Karataev was about fifty, judging by the number of campaigns in which he had served; he could not have told his exact age himself, and when he laughed, as he often did, he showed two rows of strong, white teeth. There was not a grey hair on his head or in his beard, and his bearing wore the stamp of activity, resolution, and above all, stoicism. His face, though much lined, had a touching expression of simplicity, youth, and innocence. When he spoke, in his soft sing-song voice, his speech flowed as from a well-spring. He never thought about what he had said or was going to say next, and the vivacity and the rhythmical inflections of his voice gave it a penetrating persuasiveness. Night and morning, when going to rest or getting up, he said, 'O God, let me sleep like a stone and rise up like a loaf.' And, sure enough, he had no sooner lain down than he slept like a lump of lead, and in the morning on waking he was bright and lively, and ready for any work. He could do anything, just not very well nor very ill; he cooked, sewed, planed wood, cobbled his boots, and was always occupied with some job or other, only allowing himself to chat and sing at night. He sang, not like a singer who knows he has listeners, but as the birds sing to God, the Father of all, feeling it as necessary as walking or stretching himself. His singing was tender, sweet, plaintive, almost feminine, in keeping with his serious countenance. When, after some weeks of captivity his beard had grown again, he seemed to have got rid of all that was not his true self, the borrowed face which his soldiering life had given him, and to have become, as before, a peasant and a man of the people. In the eyes of the other prisoners Plato was just a common soldier, whom they chaffed at times and sent on all manner of errands; but to Pierre he remained ever after the personification of simplicity and truth, such as he had divined him to be since the first night spent by his side."

This clearly is a study from life, a leaf from Tolstoy's "Crimean Journal." It harmonises with the point of view revealed in the "Letters from Sebastopol" (especially in the second and third series), and shows, like them, the change effected by the realities of war in the intolerant young aristocrat, who previously excluded all but the comme-il-faut from his consideration. With widened outlook and new ideals he returned to St. Petersburg at the close of the Crimean campaign, to be welcomed by the elite of letters and courted by society. A few years before he would have been delighted with such a reception. Now it jarred on his awakened sense of the tragedy of existence. He found himself entirely out of sympathy with the group of literary men who gathered round him, with Turgenev at their head. In Tolstoy's eyes they were false, paltry, and immoral, and he was at no pains to disguise his opinions. Dissension, leading to violent scenes, soon broke out between Turgenev and Tolstoy; and the latter, completely disillusioned both in regard to his great contemporary and to the literary world of St. Petersburg, shook off the dust of the capital, and, after resigning his commission in the army, went abroad on a tour through Germany, Switzerland, and France.

In France his growing aversion from capital punishment became intensified by his witnessing a public execution, and the painful thoughts aroused by the scene of the guillotine haunted his sensitive spirit for long. He left France for Switzerland, and there, among beautiful natural surroundings, and in the society of friends, he enjoyed a respite from mental strain.

"A fresh, sweet-scented flower seemed to have blossomed in my spirit; to the weariness and indifference to all things which before possessed me had succeeded, without apparent transition, a thirst for love, a confident hope, an inexplicable joy to feel myself alive."

Those halcyon days ushered in the dawn of an intimate friendship between himself and a lady who in the correspondence which ensued usually styled herself his aunt, but was in fact a second cousin. This lady, the Countess Alexandra A. Tolstoy, a Maid of Honour of the Bedchamber, moved exclusively in Court circles. She was intelligent and sympathetic, but strictly orthodox and mondaine, so that, while Tolstoy's view of life gradually shifted from that of an aristocrat to that of a social reformer, her own remained unaltered; with the result that at the end of some forty years of frank and affectionate interchange of ideas, they awoke to the painful consciousness that the last link of mutual understanding had snapped and that their friendship was at an end.

But the letters remain as a valuable and interesting record of one of Tolstoy's rare friendships with women, revealing in his unguarded confidences fine shades of his many-sided nature, and throwing light on the impression he made both on his intimates and on those to whom he was only known as a writer, while his moral philosophy was yet in embryo. They are now about to appear in book form under the auspices of M. Stakhovich, to whose kindness in giving me free access to the originals I am indebted for the extracts which follow. From one of the countess's first letters we learn that the feelings of affection, hope, and happiness which possessed Tolstoy in Switzerland irresistibly communicated themselves to those about him.

"You are good in a very uncommon way," she writes, "and that is why it is difficult to feel unhappy in your company. I have never seen you without wishing to be a better creature. Your presence is a consoling idea . . . know all the elements in you that revive one's heart, possibly without your being even aware of it."

A few years later she gives him an amusing account of the impression his writings had already made on an eminent statesman.

"I owe you a small episode. Not long ago, when lunching with the Emperor, I sat next our little Bismarck, and in a spirit of mischief I began sounding him about you. But I had hardly uttered your name when he went off at a gallop with the greatest enthusiasm, firing off the list of your perfections left and right, and so long as he declaimed your praises with gesticulations, cut and thrust, powder and shot, it was all very well and quite in character; but seeing that I listened with interest and attention my man took the bit in his teeth, and flung himself into a psychic apotheosis. On reaching full pitch he began to get muddled, and floundered so helplessly in his own phrases! all the while chewing an excellent cutlet to the bone, that at last I realised nothing but the tips of his ears—those two great ears of his. What a pity I can't repeat it verbatim! but how? There was nothing left but a jumble of confused sounds and broken words."

Tolstoy on his side is equally expansive, and in the early stages of the correspondence falls occasionally into the vein of self-analysis which in later days became habitual.

"As a child I believed with passion and without any thought. Then at the age of fourteen I began to think about life and preoccupied myself with religion, but it did not adjust itself to my theories and so I broke with it. Without it I was able to live quite contentedly for ten years . . . everything in my life was evenly distributed, and there was no room for religion. Then came a time when everything grew intelligible; there were no more secrets in life, but life itself had lost its significance."

He goes on to tell of the two years that he spent in the Caucasus before the Crimean War, when his mind, jaded by youthful excesses, gradually regained its freshness, and he awoke to a sense of communion with Nature which he retained to his life's end.

"I have my notes of that time, and now reading them over I am not able to understand how a man could attain to the state of mental exaltation which I arrived at. It was a torturing but a happy time."

Further on he writes,—"In those two years of intellectual work, I discovered a truth which is ancient and simple, but which yet I know better than others do. I found out that immortal life is a reality, that love is a reality, and that one must live for others if one would be unceasingly happy."

At this point one realises the gulf which divides the Slavonic from the English temperament. No average Englishman of seven-and-twenty (as Tolstoy was then) would pursue reflections of this kind, or if he did, he would in all probability keep them sedulously to himself.

To Tolstoy and his aunt, on the contrary, it seemed the most natural thing in the world to indulge in egoistic abstractions and to expatiate on them; for a Russian feels none of the Anglo-Saxon's mauvaise honte in describing his spiritual condition, and is no more daunted by metaphysics than the latter is by arguments on politics and sport.

To attune the Anglo-Saxon reader's mind to sympathy with a mentality so alien to his own, requires that Tolstoy's environment should be described more fully than most of his biographers have cared to do. This prefatory note aims, therefore, at being less strictly biographical than illustrative of the contributory elements and circumstances which subconsciously influenced Tolstoy's spiritual evolution, since it is apparent that in order to judge a man's actions justly one must be able to appreciate the motives from which they spring; those motives in turn requiring the key which lies in his temperament, his associations, his nationality. Such a key is peculiarly necessary to English or American students of Tolstoy, because of the marked contrast existing between the Russian and the Englishman or American in these respects, a contrast by which Tolstoy himself was forcibly struck during the visit to Switzerland, of which mention has been already made. It is difficult to restrain a smile at the poignant mental discomfort endured by the sensitive Slav in the company of the frigid and silent English frequenters of the Schweitzerhof ("Journal of Prince D. Nekhludov," Lucerne, 1857), whose reserve, he realised, was "not based on pride, but on the absence of any desire to draw nearer to each other"; while he looked back regretfully to the pension in Paris where the table d' hote was a scene of spontaneous gaiety. The problem of British taciturnity passed his comprehension; but for us the enigma of Tolstoy's temperament is half solved if we see him not harshly silhouetted against a blank wall, but suffused with his native atmosphere, amid his native surroundings. Not till we understand the main outlines of the Russian temperament can we realise the individuality of Tolstoy himself: the personality that made him lovable, the universality that made him great.

So vast an agglomeration of races as that which constitutes the Russian empire cannot obviously be represented by a single type, but it will suffice for our purposes to note the characteristics of the inhabitants of Great Russia among whom Tolstoy spent the greater part of his lifetime and to whom he belonged by birth and natural affinities.

It may be said of the average Russian that in exchange for a precocious childhood he retains much of a child's lightness of heart throughout his later years, alternating with attacks of morbid despondency. He is usually very susceptible to feminine charm, an ardent but unstable lover, whose passions are apt to be as shortlived as they are violent. Storytelling and long-winded discussions give him keen enjoyment, for he is garrulous, metaphysical, and argumentative. In money matters careless and extravagant, dilatory and venal in affairs; fond, especially in the peasant class, of singing, dancing, and carousing; but his irresponsible gaiety and heedlessness of consequences balanced by a fatalistic courage and endurance in the face of suffering and danger. Capable, besides, of high flights of idealism, which result in epics, but rarely in actions, owing to the Slavonic inaptitude for sustained and organised effort. The Englishman by contrast appears cold and calculating, incapable of rising above questions of practical utility; neither interested in other men's antecedents and experiences nor willing to retail his own. The catechism which Plato puts Pierre through on their first encounter ("War and Peace") as to his family, possessions, and what not, are precisely similar to those to which I have been subjected over and over again by chance acquaintances in country-houses or by fellow travellers on journeys by boat or train. The naivete and kindliness of the questioner makes it impossible to resent, though one may feebly try to parry his probing. On the other hand he offers you free access to the inmost recesses of his own soul, and stupefies you with the candour of his revelations. This, of course, relates more to the landed and professional classes than to the peasant, who is slower to express himself, and combines in a curious way a firm belief in the omnipotence and wisdom of his social superiors with a rooted distrust of their intentions regarding himself. He is like a beast of burden who flinches from every approach, expecting always a kick or a blow. On the other hand, his affection for the animals who share his daily work is one of the most attractive points in his character, and one which Tolstoy never wearied of emphasising—describing, with the simple pathos of which he was master, the moujik inured to his own privations but pitiful to his horse, shielding him from the storm with his own coat, or saving him from starvation with his own meagre ration; and mindful of him even in his prayers, invoking, like Plato, the blessings of Florus and Laura, patron saints of horses, because "one mustn't forget the animals."

The characteristics of a people so embedded in the soil bear a closer relation to their native landscape than our own migratory populations, and patriotism with them has a deep and vital meaning, which is expressed unconsciously in their lives.

This spirit of patriotism which Tolstoy repudiated is none the less the animating power of the noble epic, "War and Peace," and of his peasant-tales, of his rare gift of reproducing the expressive Slav vernacular, and of his magical art of infusing his pictures of Russian scenery not merely with beauty, but with spiritual significance. I can think of no prose writer, unless it be Thoreau, so wholly under the spell of Nature as Tolstoy; and while Thoreau was preoccupied with the normal phenomena of plant and animal life, Tolstoy, coming near to Pantheism, found responses to his moods in trees, and gained spiritual expansion from the illimitable skies and plains. He frequently brings his heroes into touch with Nature, and endows them with all the innate mysticism of his own temperament, for to him Nature was "a guide to God." So in the twofold incident of Prince Andre and the oak tree ("War and Peace") the

Prince, though a man of action rather than of sentiment and habitually cynical, is ready to find in the aged oak by the roadside, in early spring, an animate embodiment of his own despondency.

"'Springtime, love, happiness?—are you still cherishing those deceptive illusions?' the old oak seemed to say. 'Isn't it the same fiction ever? There is neither spring, nor love, nor happiness! Look at those poor weather-beaten firs, always the same . . . look at the knotty arms issuing from all up my poor mutilated trunk—here I am, such as they have made me, and I do not believe either in your hopes or in your illusions.'"

And after thus exercising his imagination, Prince Andre still casts backward glances as he passes by, "but the oak maintained its obstinate and sullen immovability in the midst of the flowers and grass growing at its feet. 'Yes, that oak is right, right a thousand times over. One must leave illusions to youth. But the rest of us know what life is worth; it has nothing left to offer us.'"

Six weeks later he returns homeward the same way, roused from his melancholy torpor by his recent meeting with Natasha.

"The day was hot, there was storm in the air; a slight shower watered the dust on the road and the grass in the ditch; the left side of the wood remained in the shade; the right side, lightly stirred by the wind, glittered all wet in the sun; everything was in flower, and from near and far the nightingales poured forth their song. 'I fancy there was an oak here that understood me,' said Prince Andre to himself, looking to the left and attracted unawares by the beauty of the very tree he sought. The transformed old oak spread out in a dome of deep, luxuriant, blooming verdure, which swayed in a light breeze in the rays of the setting sun. There were no longer cloven branches nor rents to be seen; its former aspect of bitter defiance and sullen grief had disappeared; there were only the young leaves, full of sap that had pierced through the centenarian bark, making the beholder question with surprise if this patriarch had really given birth to them. 'Yes, it is he, indeed!' cried Prince Andre, and he felt his heart suffused by the intense joy which the springtime and this new life gave him . . . 'No, my life cannot end at thirty-one! . . . It is not enough myself to feel what is within me, others must know it too! Pierre and that "slip" of a girl, who would have fled into cloudland, must learn to know me! My life must colour theirs, and their lives must mingle with mine!'"

In letters to his wife, to intimate friends, and in his diary, Tolstoy's love of Nature is often-times expressed. The hair shirt of the ascetic and the prophet's mantle fall from his shoulders, and all the poet in him wakes when, "with a feeling akin to ecstasy," he looks up from his smooth-running sledge at "the enchanting, starry winter sky overhead," or in early spring feels on a ramble "intoxicated by the beauty of the morning," while he notes that the buds are swelling on the lilacs, and "the birds no longer sing at random," but have begun to converse.

But though such allusions abound in his diary and private correspondence, we must turn to "The Cossacks," and "Conjugal Happiness" for the exquisitely elaborated rural studies, which give those early romances their fresh idyllic charm.

What is interesting to note is that this artistic freshness and joy in Nature coexisted with acute intermittent attacks of spiritual lassitude. In "The Cossacks," the doubts, the mental gropings of Olenine—whose personality but thinly veils that of Tolstoy—haunt him betimes even among the delights of the Caucasian woodland; Serge, the fatalistic hero of "Conjugal Happiness," calmly acquiesces in the inevitableness of "love's sad satiety" amid the scent of roses and the songs of nightingales.

Doubt and despondency, increased by the vexations and failures attending his philanthropic endeavours, at length obsessed Tolstoy to the verge of suicide.

"The disputes over arbitration had become so painful to me, the schoolwork so vague, my doubts arising from the wish to teach others, while dissembling my own ignorance of what should be taught, were so heartrending that I fell ill. I might then have reached the despair to which I all but succumbed fifteen years later, if there had not been a side of life as yet unknown to me which promised me salvation: this was family life" ("My Confession").

In a word, his marriage with Mademoiselle Sophie Andreevna Bers (daughter of Dr. Bers of Moscow) was consummated in the autumn of 1862—after a somewhat protracted courtship, owing to her extreme youth—and Tolstoy entered upon a period of happiness and mental peace such as he had never known. His letters of this period to Countess A. A. Tolstoy, his friend Fet, and others, ring with enraptured allusions to his new-found joy. Lassitude and indecision, mysticism and altruism, all were swept aside by the impetus of triumphant love and of all-sufficing conjugal happiness. When in June of the following year a child was born, and the young wife, her features suffused with "a supernatural beauty" lay trying to smile at the husband who knelt sobbing beside her, Tolstoy must have realised that for once his prophetic intuition had been unequal to its task. If his imagination could have conceived in prenuptial days what depths of emotion might be wakened by fatherhood, he would not have treated the birth of Masha's first child in "Conjugal Happiness" as a trivial material event, in no way affecting the mutual relations of the disillusioned pair. He would have understood that at this supreme crisis, rather than in the vernal hour of love's avowal, the heart is illumined with a joy which is fated "never to return."

The parting of the ways, so soon reached by Serge and Masha, was in fact delayed in Tolstoy's own life by his wife's intelligent assistance in his literary work as an untiring amanuensis, and in the mutual anxieties and pleasures attending the care of a large family of young children. Wider horizons opened to his mental vision, his whole being was quickened and invigorated. "War and Peace," "Anna Karenina," all the splendid fruit of the teeming years following upon his marriage, bear witness to the stimulus which his genius had received. His dawning recognition of the power and extent of female influence appears incidentally in the sketches of high society in those two masterpieces as well as in the eloquent closing passages of "What then must we do?" (1886). Having affirmed that "it is women who form public opinion, and in our day women are particularly powerful," he finally draws a picture of the ideal wife who shall urge her husband and train her children to self-sacrifice. "Such women rule men and are their guiding stars. O women—mothers! The salvation of the world lies in your hands!" In that appeal to the mothers of the world there lurks a protest which in later writings developed into overwhelming condemnation. True, he chose motherhood for the type of self-sacrificing love in the treatise "On Life," which appeared soon after "What then must we do?" but maternal love, as exemplified in his own home and elsewhere, appeared to him as a noble instinct perversely directed.

The roots of maternal love are sunk deep in conservatism. The child's physical well-being is the first essential in the mother's eyes—the growth of a vigorous body by which a vigorous mind may be fitly tenanted—and this form of materialism which Tolstoy as a father accepted, Tolstoy as idealist condemned; while the penury he courted as a lightening of his soul's burden was averted by the strenuous exertions of his wife. So a rift grew without blame attaching to either, and Tolstoy henceforward wandered solitary in spirit through a wilderness of thought, seeking rest and finding none, coming perilously near to suicide before he reached haven.

To many it will seem that the finest outcome of that period of mental groping, internal struggle, and contending with current ideas, lies in the above-mentioned "What then must we do?" Certain it is that no human document ever revealed the soul of its author with greater sincerity. Not for its practical suggestions, but for its impassioned humanity, its infectious altruism, "What then must we do?" takes its rank among the world's few living books. It marks that stage of Tolstoy's evolution when he made successive essays in practical philanthropy which filled him with discouragement, yet were "of use to his soul" in teaching him how far below the surface lie the seeds of human misery. The slums of Moscow, crowded with beings sunk beyond redemption; the famine-stricken plains of Samara where disease and starvation reigned, notwithstanding the stream of charity set flowing by Tolstoy's appeals and notwithstanding his untiring personal devotion, strengthened further the conviction, so constantly affirmed in his writings, of the impotence of money to alleviate distress. Whatever negations of this dictum our own systems of charitable organizations may appear to offer, there can be no question but that in Russia it held and holds true.

The social condition of Russia is like a tideless sea, whose sullen quiescence is broken from time to time by terrific storms which spend themselves in unavailing fury. Reaction follows upon every forward motion, and the advance made by each succeeding generation is barely perceptible.

But in the period of peace following upon the close of the Crimean War the soul of the Russian people was deeply stirred by the spirit of Progress, and hope rose high on the accession of Alexander II.

The emancipation of the serfs was only one among a number of projected reforms which engaged men's minds. The national conscience awoke and echoed the cry of the exiled patriot Herzen, "Now or never!" Educational enterprise was aroused, and some forty schools for peasant children were started on the model of that opened by Tolstoy at Yasnaya Polyana (1861). The literary world throbbed with new life, and a brilliant company of young writers came to the surface, counting among them names of European celebrity, such as Dostoevsky, Nekrassov, and Saltykov. Unhappily the reign of Progress was short. The bureaucratic circle hemming in the Czar took alarm, and made haste to secure their ascendancy by fresh measures of oppression. Many schools were closed, including that of Tolstoy, and the nascent liberty of the Press was stifled by the most rigid censorship.

In this lamentable manner the history of Russia's internal misrule and disorder has continued to repeat itself for the last sixty years, revolving in the same vicious circle of fierce repression and persecution and utter disregard of the rights of individuals, followed by fierce reprisals on the part of the persecuted; the voice of protest no sooner raised than silenced in a prison cell or among Siberian snow-fields, yet rising again and again with inextinguishable reiteration; appeals for political freedom, for constitutional government, for better systems and wider dissemination of education, for liberty of the Press, and for an enlightened treatment of the masses, callously received and rejected. The answer with which these appeals have been met by the rulers of Russia is only too well known to the civilised world, but the obduracy of Pharoah has called forth the plagues of Egypt. Despite the unrivalled agrarian fertility of Russia, famines recur with dire frequency, with disease and riot in their train, while the ignominious termination of the Russo-Japanese war showed that even the magnificent morale of the Russian soldier had been undermined and was tainted by the rottenness of the authorities set over him. What in such circumstances as these can a handful of philanthropists achieve, and what avails alms-giving or the scattering of largesse to a people on the point of spiritual dissolution?

In these conditions Tolstoy's abhorrence of money, and his assertion of its futility as a panacea for human suffering, appears not merely comprehensible but inevitable, and his renunciation of personal property the strictly logical outcome of his conclusions. The partition of his estates between his wife and children, shortly before the outbreak of the great famine in 1892, served to relieve his mind partially; and the writings of Henry George, with which he became acquainted at this critical time, were an additional incentive to concentrate his thoughts on the land question. He began by reading the American propagandist's "Social Problems," which arrested his attention by its main principles and by the clearness and novelty of his arguments. Deeply impressed by the study of this book, no sooner had he finished it than he possessed himself of its forerunner, "Progress and Poverty," in which the essence of George's revolutionary doctrines is worked out.

The plan of land nationalisation there explained provided Tolstoy with well thought-out and logical reasons for a policy that was already more than sympathetic to him. Here at last was a means of ensuring economic equality for all, from the largest landowner to the humblest peasant—a practical suggestion how to reduce the inequalities between rich and poor.

Henry George's ideas and methods are easy of comprehension. The land was made by God for every human creature that was born into the world, and therefore to confine the ownership of land to the few is wrong. If a man wants a piece of land, he ought to pay the rest of the community for the enjoyment of it. This payment or rent should be the only tax paid into the Treasury of the State. Taxation on men's own property (the produce of their own labour) should be done away with, and a rent graduated according to the site-value of the land should be substituted. Monopolies would cease without violently and unjustly disturbing society with confiscation and redistribution. No one would keep land idle if he were taxed according to its value to the community, and not according to the use to which he individually wished to put it. A man would then readily obtain possession of land, and could turn it to account and develop it without being taxed on his own industry. All human beings would thus become free in their lives and in their labour. They would no longer be forced to toil at demoralising work for low wages; they would be independent producers instead of earning a living by providing luxuries for the rich, who had enslaved them by monopolising the land. The single tax thus created would ultimately overthrow the present "civilisation" which is chiefly built up on wage-slavery.

Tolstoy gave his whole-hearted adhesion to this doctrine, predicting a day of enlightenment when men would no longer tolerate a form of slavery which he considered as revolting as that which had so recently been abolished. Some long conversations with Henry George, while he was on a visit to Yasnaya Polyana, gave additional strength to Tolstoy's conviction that in these theories lay the elements essential to the transformation and rejuvenation of human nature, going far towards the levelling of social inequalities. But to inoculate the landed proprietors of Russia as a class with those theories was a task which even his genius could not hope to accomplish.

He recognised the necessity of proceeding from the particular to the general, and that the perfecting of human institutions was impossible without a corresponding perfection in the individual. To this end therefore the remainder of his life was dedicated. He had always held in aversion what he termed external epidemic influences: he now endeavoured to free himself not only from all current conventions, but from every association which he had formerly cherished. Self-analysis and general observation had taught him that men are sensual beings, and that sensualism must die for want of food if it were not for sex instincts, if it were not for Art, and especially for Music. This view of life he forcibly expressed in the "Kreutzer Sonata," in which Woman and Music, the two magnets of his youth, were impeached as powers of evil. Already, in "War and Peace" and in "Anna Karenina," his descriptions of female charms resembled catalogues of weapons against which a man must arm himself or perish. The beautiful Princess Helena, with her gleaming shoulders, her faultless white bosom, and her eternal smile is evidently an object of aversion to her creator; even as the Countess Betsy, with her petty coquetries and devices for attracting attention at the Opera and elsewhere, is a target for his contempt. "Woman is a stumbling-block in a man's career," remarks a philosophical husband in "Anna Karenina." "It is difficult to love a woman and do any good work, and the only way to escape being reduced to inaction is to marry."

Even in his correspondence with the Countess A. A. Tolstoy this slighting tone prevails. "A woman has but one moral weapon instead of the whole male arsenal. That is love, and only with this weapon is feminine education successfully carried forward." Tolstoy, in fact, betrayed a touch of orientalism in his attitude towards women. In part no doubt as a result of his motherless youth, in part to the fact that his idealism was never stimulated by any one woman as it was by individual men, his views retained this colouring on sex questions while they became widened and modified in almost every other field of human philosophy. It was only that, with a revulsion of feeling not seldom experienced by earnest thinkers, attraction was succeeded by a repulsion which reached the high note of exasperation when he wrote to a man friend, "A woman in good health—why, she is a regular beast of prey!"

None the less, he showed great kindness and sympathy to the women who sought his society, appealing to him for guidance. One of these (an American, and herself a practical philanthropist), Miss Jane Addams, expressed with feeling her sense of his personal influence. "The glimpse of Tolstoy has made a profound impression on me, not so much by what he said, as the life, the gentleness, the soul of him. I am sure you will understand my saying that I got more of Tolstoy's philosophy from our conversations than I had gotten from our books." (Quoted by Aylmer Maude in his "Life of Tolstoy.")

As frequently happens in the lives of reformers, Tolstoy found himself more often in affinity with strangers than with his own kin. The estrangement of his ideals from those of his wife necessarily affected their conjugal relations, and the decline of mutual sympathy inevitably induced physical alienation. The stress of mental anguish arising from these conditions found vent in pages of his diaries (much of which I have been permitted to read), pages containing matter too sacred and intimate to use. The diaries shed a flood of light on Tolstoy's ideas, motives, and manner of life, and have modified some of my opinions, explaining many hitherto obscure points, while they have also enhanced my admiration for the man. They not only touch on many delicate subjects—on his relations to his wife and family—but they also give the true reasons for leaving his home at last, and explain why he did not do so before. The time, it seems to me, is not ripe for disclosures of this nature, which so closely concern the living.

Despite a strong rein of restraint his mental distress permeates the touching letter of farewell which he wrote some sixteen years before his death. He, however, shrank from acting upon it, being unable to satisfy himself that it was a right step. This letter has already appeared in foreign publications,[1] but it is quoted here because "I have suffered long, dear Sophie, from the discord between my life and my beliefs.

"I cannot constrain you to alter your life or your accustomed ways. Neither have I had the strength to leave you ere this, for I thought my absence might deprive the little ones, still so young, of whatever influence I may have over them, and above all that I should grieve you. But I can no longer live as I have lived these last sixteen years, sometimes battling with you and irritating you, sometimes myself giving way to the influences and seductions to which I am accustomed and which surround me. I have now resolved to do what I have long desired: to go away . . . Even as the Hindoos, at the age of sixty, betake themselves to the jungle; even as every aged and religious-minded man desires to consecrate the last years of his life to God and not to idle talk, to making jokes, to gossiping, to lawn-tennis; so I, having reached the age of seventy, long with all my soul for calm and solitude, and if not perfect harmony, at least a cessation from this horrible discord between my whole life and my conscience.

"If I had gone away openly there would have been entreaties, discussions: I should have wavered, and perhaps failed to act on my decision, whereas it must be so. I pray of you to forgive me if my action grieves you. And do you, Sophie, in particular let me go, neither seeking me out, nor bearing me ill-will, nor blaming me . . . the fact that I have left you does not mean that I have cause of complaint against you . . . I know you were not able, you were incapable of thinking and seeing as I do, and therefore you could not change your life and make sacrifices to that which you did not accept. Besides, I do not blame you; on the contrary, I remember with love and gratitude the thirty-five long years of our life in common, and especially the first half of the time when,

---

[1]   And in Birukov's short Life of Tolstoy, 1911. of the light which it throws on the character and disposition of the writer, the workings of his mind being of greater moment to us than those impulsive actions by which he was too often judged.

with the courage and devotion of your maternal nature, you bravely bore what you regarded as your mission. You have given largely of maternal love and made some heavy sacrifices . . . but during the latter part of our life together, during the last fifteen years, our ways have parted. I cannot think myself the guilty one; I know that if I have changed it is not owing to you, or to the world, but because I could not do otherwise; nor can I judge you for not having followed me, and I thank you for what you have given me and will ever remember it with affection.

"Adieu, my dear Sophie, I love you."

The personal isolation he craved was never to be his; but the isolation of spirit essential to leadership, whether of thought or action, grew year by year, so that in his own household he was veritably "in it but not of it."

At times his loneliness weighed upon him, as when he wrote: "You would find it difficult to imagine how isolated I am, to what an extent my true self is despised by those who surround me." But he must, none the less, have realised, as all prophets and seers have done, that solitariness of soul and freedom from the petty complexities of social life are necessary to the mystic whose constant endeavour is to simplify and to winnow, the transient from the eternal.

Notwithstanding the isolation of his inner life he remained—or it might more accurately be said he became—the most accessible of men.

Appeals for guidance came to him from all parts of the world—America, France, China, Japan—while Yasnaya Polyana was the frequent resort of those needing advice, sympathy, or practical assistance. None appealed to him in vain; at the same time, he was exceedingly chary of explicit rules of conduct. It might be said of Tolstoy that he became a spiritual leader in spite of himself, so averse was he from assuming authority. His aim was ever to teach his followers themselves to hear the inward monitory voice, and to obey it of their own accord. "To know the meaning of Life, you must first know the meaning of Love," he would say; "and then see that you do what love bids you." His distrust of "epidemic ideas" extended to religious communities and congregations.

"We must not go to meet each other, but go each of us to God. You say it is easier to go all together? Why yes, to dig or to mow. But one can only draw near to God in isolation . . . I picture the world to myself as a vast temple, in which the light falls from above in the very centre. To meet together all must go towards the light. There we shall find ourselves, gathered from many quarters, united with men we did not expect to see; therein is joy."

The humility which had so completely supplanted his youthful arrogance, and which made him shrink from impelling others to follow in his steps, endued him also with the teachableness of a child towards those whom he accepted as his spiritual mentors. It was a peasant nonconformist writer, Soutaev, who by conversing with him on the revelations of the Gospels helped him to regain his childhood's faith, and incidentally brought him into closer relations with religious, but otherwise untaught, men of the people. He saw how instead of railing against fate after the manner of their social superiors, they endured sickness and misfortune with a calm confidence that all was by the will of God, as it must be and should be. From his peasant teachers he drew the watchwords Faith, Love, and Labour, and by their light he established that concord in his own life without which the concord of the universe remains impossible to realise. The process of inward struggle—told with unsparing truth in "Confession"—is finely painted in "Father Serge," whose life story points to the conclusion at which Tolstoy ultimately arrived, namely, that not in withdrawal from the common trials and temptations of men, but in sharing them, lies our best fulfilment of our duty towards mankind and towards God. Tolstoy gave practical effect to this principle, and to this long-felt desire to be of use to the poor of the country, by editing and publishing, aided by his friend Chertkov,[2] modern literature has awakened so universal a sense of sympathy and admiration, perhaps because none has been so entirely a labour of love.

2   In Russia and out of it Mr. Chertkov has been the subject of violent attack. Many of the misunderstandings of Tolstoy's later years have also been attributed by critics, and by those who hate or belittle his ideas, to the influence of this friend. These attacks are very regrettable and require a word of protest. From tales, suited to the means and intelligence of the humblest peasant. The undertaking was initiated in 1885, and continued for many years to occupy much of Tolstoy's time and energies. He threw himself with ardour into his editorial duties; reading and correcting manuscripts, returning them sometimes to the authors with advice as to their reconstruction, and making translations from foreign works—all this in addition to his own original contributions, in which he carried out the principle which he constantly laid down for his collaborators, that literary graces must be set aside, and that the mental calibre of those for whom the books were primarily intended must be constantly borne in mind. He attained a splendid fulfilment of his own theories, employing the moujik's expressive vernacular in portraying his homely wisdom, religious faith, and goodness of nature. Sometimes the prevailing simplicity of style and motive is tinged with a vague colouring of oriental legend, but the personal accent is marked throughout. No similar achievement in the beginning Mr. Chertkov has striven to spread the ideas of Tolstoy, and has won neither glory nor money from his faithful and single-hearted devotion. He has carried on his work with a rare love and sympathy in spite of difficulties. No one appreciated or valued his friendship and self-sacrifice more than Tolstoy himself, who was firmly attached to him from the date of his first meeting, consulting him and confiding in him at every moment, even during Mr. Chertkov's long exile.

The series of educational primers which Tolstoy prepared and published concurrently with the "Popular Tales" have had an equally large, though exclusively Russian, circulation, being admirably suited to their purpose—that of teaching young children the rudiments of history, geography, and science. Little leisure remained for the service of Art.

The history of Tolstoy as a man of letters forms a separate page of his biography, and one into which it is not possible to enter in the brief compass of this introduction. It requires, however, a passing allusion. Tolstoy even in his early days never seems to have approached near to that manner of life which the literary man leads: neither to have shut himself up in his study, nor to have barred the entrance to disturbing friends. On the one hand, he was fond of society, and during his brief residence in St. Petersburg was never so engrossed in authorship as to forego the pleasure of a ball or evening entertainment. Little wonder, when one looks back at the brilliant young officer surrounded and petted by the great hostesses of Russia. On the other hand, he was no devotee at the literary altar. No patron of literature could claim him as his constant visitor; no inner circle of men of letters monopolised his idle hours. Afterwards, when he left the capital and settled in the country, he was almost entirely cut off from the association of literary men, and never seems to have sought their companionship. Nevertheless, he had all through his life many fast friends, among them such as the poet Fet, the novelist Chekhov, and the great Russian librarian Stassov, who often came to him. These visits always gave him pleasure. The discussions, whether on the literary movements of the day or on the merits of Goethe or the humour of Gogol, were welcome interruptions to his ever-absorbing metaphysical studies. In later life, also, though never in touch with the rising generation of authors, we find him corresponding with them, criticising their style and subject matter. When Andreev, the most modern of all modern Russian writers, came to pay his respects to Tolstoy some months before his death, he was received with cordiality, although Tolstoy, as he expressed himself afterwards, felt that there was a great gulf fixed between them.

Literature, as literature, had lost its charm for him. "You are perfectly right," he writes to a friend; "I care only for the idea, and I pay no attention to my style." The idea was the important thing to Tolstoy in everything that he read or wrote. When his attention was drawn to an illuminating essay on the poet Lermontov he was pleased with it, not because it demonstrated Lermontov's position in the literary history of Russia, but because it pointed out the moral aims which underlay the wild Byronism of his works. He reproached the novelist Leskov, who had sent him his latest novel, for the "exuberance" of his flowers of speech and for his florid sentences—beautiful in their way, he says, but inexpedient and unnecessary. He even counselled the younger generation to give up poetry as a form of expression and to use prose instead. Poetry, he maintained, was always artificial and obscure. His attitude towards the art of writing remained to the end one of hostility. Whenever he caught himself working for art he was wont to reproach himself, and his diaries contain many recriminations against his own weakness in yielding to this besetting temptation. Yet to these very lapses we are indebted for this collection of fragments.

The greater number of stories and plays contained in these volumes date from the years following upon Tolstoy's pedagogic activity. Long intervals, however, elapsed in most cases between the original synopsis and the final touches. Thus "Father Serge," of which he sketched the outline to Mr. Chertkov in 1890, was so often put aside to make way for purely ethical writings that not till 1898 does the entry occur in his diary, "To-day, quite unexpectedly, I finished Serge." A year previously a dramatic incident had come to his knowledge, which he elaborated in the play entitled "The Man who was dead." It ran on the lines familiarised by Enoch Arden and similar stories, of a wife deserted by her husband and supported in his absence by a benefactor, whom she subsequently marries. In this instance the supposed dead man was suddenly resuscitated as the result of his own admissions in his cups, the wife and her second husband being consequently arrested and condemned to a term of imprisonment. Tolstoy seriously attacked the subject during the summer of 1900, and having brought it within a measurable distance of completion in a shorter time than was usual with him, submitted it to the judgment of a circle of friends. The drama made a deep impression on the privileged few who read it, and some mention of it appeared in the newspapers.

Shortly afterwards a young man came to see Tolstoy in private. He begged him to refrain from publishing "The Man who was dead," as it was the history of his mother's life, and would distress her gravely, besides possibly occasioning further police intervention. Tolstoy promptly consented, and the play remained, as it now appears, in an unfinished condition. He had already felt doubtful whether "it was a thing God would approve," Art for Art's sake having in his eyes no right to existence. For this reason a didactic tendency is increasingly evident in these later stories. "After the Ball" gives a painful picture of Russian military cruelty; "The Forged Coupon" traces the cancerous growth of evil, and demonstrates with dramatic force the cumulative misery resulting from one apparently trivial act of wrongdoing.

Of the three plays included in these volumes, "The Light that shines in Darkness" has a special claim to our attention as an example of autobiography in the guise of drama. It is a specimen of Tolstoy's gift of seeing himself as others saw him, and viewing a question in all its bearings. It presents not actions but ideas, giving with entire impartiality the opinions of his home circle, of his friends, of the Church and of the State, in regard to his altruistic propaganda and to the anarchism of which he has been accused. The scene of the renunciation of the estates of the hero may be taken as a literal version of what actually took place in regard to Tolstoy himself, while the dialogues by which the piece is carried forward are more like verbatim records than imaginary conversations.

This play was, in addition, a medium by which Tolstoy emphasised his abhorrence of military service, and probably for this reason its production is absolutely forbidden in Russia. A word may be said here on Tolstoy's so-called Anarchy, a term admitting of grave misconstruction. In that he denied the benefit of existing governments to the people over whom they ruled, and in that he stigmatised standing armies as "collections of disciplined murderers," Tolstoy was an Anarchist; but in that he reprobated the methods of violence, no matter how righteous the cause at stake, and upheld by word and deed the gospel of Love and submission, he cannot be judged guilty of Anarchism in its full significance. He could not, however, suppress the sympathy which he felt with those whose resistance to oppression brought them into deadly conflict with autocracy. He found in the Caucasian chieftain, Hadji Murat, a subject full of human interest and dramatic possibilities; and though some eight years passed before he corrected the manuscript for the last time (in 1903), it is evident from the numbers of entries in his diary that it had greatly occupied his thoughts so far back even as the period which he spent in Tiflis prior to the Crimean war. It was then that the final subjugation of the Caucasus took place, and Shamil and his devoted band made their last struggle for freedom. After the lapse of half a century, Tolstoy gave vent in "Hadji Murat" to the resentment which the military despotism of Nicholas I. had roused in his sensitive and fearless spirit.

Courage was the dominant note in Tolstoy's character, and none have excelled him in portraying brave men. His own fearlessness was of the rarest, in that it was both physical and moral. The mettle tried and proved at Sebastopol sustained him when he had drawn on himself the bitter animosity of "Holy Synod" and the relentless anger of Czardom. In spite of his nonresistance doctrine, Tolstoy's courage was not of the passive order. It was his natural bent to rouse his foes to combat, rather than wait for their attack, to put on the defensive every falsehood and every wrong of which he was cognisant. Truth in himself and in others was what he most desired, and that to which he strove at all costs to attain. He was his own severest critic, weighing his own actions, analysing his own thoughts, and baring himself to the eyes of the world with unflinching candour. Greatest of autobiographers, he extenuates nothing: you see the whole man with his worst faults and best qualities; weaknesses accentuated by the energy with which they are charactered, apparent waste of mental forces bent on solving the insoluble, inherited tastes and prejudices, altruistic impulses and virile passions, egoism and idealism, all strangely mingled and continually warring against each other, until from the death-throes of spiritual conflict issued a new birth and a new life. In the ancient Scripture "God is love" Tolstoy discerned fresh meaning, and strove with superhuman energy to bring home that meaning to the world at large. His doctrine in fact appears less as a new light in the darkness than as a revival of the pure flame of "the Mystic of the Galilean hills," whose teaching he accepted while denying His divinity.

Of Tolstoy's beliefs in regard to the Christian religion it may be said that with advancing years he became more and more disposed to regard religious truth as one continuous stream of spiritual thought flowing through the ages of man's history, emanating principally from the inspired prophets and seers of Israel, India, and China. Finally, in 1909, in a letter to a friend he summed up his conviction in the following words:—"For me the doctrine of Jesus is simply one of those beautiful religious doctrines which we have received from Egyptian, Jewish, Hindoo, Chinese, and Greek antiquity. The two great principles of Jesus: love of God—in a word absolute perfection—and love of one's neighbour, that is to say, love of all men without distinction, have been preached by all the sages of the world—Krishna, Buddha, Laotse, Confucius, Socrates, Plato, Epictetus, Marcus Aurelius, and among the moderns, Rousseau, Pascal, Kant, Emerson, Channing, and many others. Religious and moral truth is everywhere and always the same. I have no predilection whatever for Christianity. If I have been particularly interested in the doctrine of Jesus it is, firstly, because I was born in that religion and have lived among Christians; secondly, because I have found a great spiritual joy in freeing the doctrine in its purity from the astounding falsifications wrought by the Churches."

Tolstoy's life-work was indeed a splendid striving to free truth from falsehood, to simplify the complexities of civilisation and demonstrate their futility. Realists as gifted have come and gone and left but little trace. It is conceivable that the great trilogy of "Anna Karenina," "War and Peace," and "Resurrection" may one day be forgotten, but Tolstoy's teaching stands on firmer foundations, and has stirred the hearts of thousands who are indifferent to the finest display of psychic analysis. He has taught men to venture beyond the limits set by reason, to rise above the actual and to find the meaning of life in love. It was his mission to probe our moral ulcers to the roots and to raise moribund ideals from the dust, breathing his own vitality into them, till they rose before our eyes as living aspirations. The spiritual joy of which he wrote was no rhetorical hyperbole; it was manifest in the man himself, and was the fount of the lofty idealism which made him not only "the Conscience of Russia" but of the civilised world.

Idealism is one of those large abstractions which are invested by various minds with varying shades of meaning, and which find expression in an infinite number of forms. Ideals bred and fostered in the heart of man receive at birth an impress from the life that engenders them, and when that life is tempest-tossed the thought that springs from it must bear a birth-mark of the storm. That birth-mark is stamped on all Tolstoy's utterances, the simplest and the most metaphysical. But though he did not pass scathless through the purging fires, nor escape with eyes undimmed from the mystic light which flooded his soul, his ideal is not thereby invalidated. It was, he admitted, unattainable, but none the less a state of perfection to which we must continually aspire, undaunted by partial failure.

"There is nothing wrong in not living up to the ideal which you have made for yourself, but what is wrong is, if on looking back, you cannot see that you have made the least step nearer to your ideal."

How far Tolstoy's doctrines may influence succeeding generations it is impossible to foretell; but when time has extinguished what is merely personal or racial, the divine spark which he received from his great spiritual forerunners in other times and countries will undoubtedly be found alight. His universality enabled him to unite himself closely with them in mental sympathy; sometimes so closely, as in the case of J. J. Rousseau, as to raise analogies and comparisons designed to show that he merely followed in a well-worn pathway. Yet the similarity of Tolstoy's ideas to those of the author of the "Contrat Social" hardly goes beyond a mutual distrust of Art and Science as aids to human happiness and virtue, and a desire to establish among mankind a true sense of brotherhood. For the rest, the appeals which they individually made to Humanity were as dissimilar as the currents of their lives, and equally dissimilar in effect.

The magic flute of Rousseau's eloquence breathed fanaticism into his disciples, and a desire to mass themselves against the foes of liberty. Tolstoy's trumpet-call sounds a deeper note. It pierces the heart, summoning each man to the inquisition of his own conscience, and to justify his existence by labour, that he may thereafter sleep the sleep of peace.

The exaltation which he awakens owes nothing to rhythmical language nor to subtle interpretations of sensuous emotion; it proceeds from a perception of eternal truth, the truth that has love, faith, courage, and self-sacrifice for the cornerstones of its enduring edifice.

THE FORGED COUPON

FIRST PART

I

FEDOR MIHAILOVICH SMOKOVNIKOV, the president of the local Income Tax Department, a man of unswerving honesty—and proud of it, too—a gloomy Liberal, a free-thinker, and an enemy to every manifestation of religious feeling, which he thought a relic of superstition, came home from his office feeling very much annoyed. The Governor of the province had sent him an extraordinarily stupid minute, almost assuming that his dealings had been dishonest.

Fedor Mihailovich felt embittered, and wrote at once a sharp answer. On his return home everything seemed to go contrary to his wishes.

It was five minutes to five, and he expected the dinner to be served at once, but he was told it was not ready. He banged the door and went to his study. Somebody knocked at the door. "Who the devil is that?" he thought; and shouted,—"Who is there?"

The door opened and a boy of fifteen came in, the son of Fedor Mihailovich, a pupil of the fifth class of the local school.

"What do you want?"

"It is the first of the month to-day, father."

"Well! You want your money?"

It had been arranged that the father should pay his son a monthly allowance of three roubles as pocket money. Fedor Mihailovich frowned, took out of his pocket-book a coupon of two roubles fifty kopeks which he found among the bank-notes, and added to it fifty kopeks in silver out of the loose change in his purse. The boy kept silent, and did not take the money his father proffered him.

"Father, please give me some more in advance."

"What?"

"I would not ask for it, but I have borrowed a small sum from a friend, and promised upon my word of honour to pay it off. My honour is dear to me, and that is why I want another three roubles. I don't like asking you; but, please, father, give me another three roubles."

"I have told you—"

"I know, father, but just for once."

"You have an allowance of three roubles and you ought to be content. I had not fifty kopeks when I was your age."

"Now, all my comrades have much more. Petrov and Ivanitsky have fifty roubles a month."

"And I tell you that if you behave like them you will be a scoundrel. Mind that."

"What is there to mind? You never understand my position. I shall be disgraced if I don't pay my debt. It is all very well for you to speak as you do."

"Be off, you silly boy! Be off!"

Fedor Mihailovich jumped from his seat and pounced upon his son. "Be off, I say!" he shouted. "You deserve a good thrashing, all you boys!"

His son was at once frightened and embittered. The bitterness was even greater than the fright. With his head bent down he hastily turned to the door. Fedor Mihailovich did not intend to strike him, but he was glad to vent his wrath, and went on shouting and abusing the boy till he had closed the door.

When the maid came in to announce that dinner was ready, Fedor Mihailovich rose.

"At last!" he said. "I don't feel hungry any longer."

He went to the dining-room with a sullen face. At table his wife made some remark, but he gave her such a short and angry answer that she abstained from further speech. The son also did not lift his eyes from his plate, and was silent all the time. The trio finished their dinner in silence, rose from the table and separated, without a word.

After dinner the boy went to his room, took the coupon and the change out of his pocket, and threw the money on the table. After that he took off his uniform and put on a jacket.

He sat down to work, and began to study Latin grammar out of a dog's-eared book. After a while he rose, closed and bolted the door, shifted the money into a drawer, took out some cigarette papers, rolled one up, stuffed it with cotton wool, and began to smoke.

He spent nearly two hours over his grammar and writing books without understanding a word of what he saw before him; then he rose and began to stamp up and down the room, trying to recollect all that his father had said to him. All the abuse showered upon him, and worst of all his father's angry face, were as fresh in his memory as if he saw and heard them all over again. "Silly boy! You ought to get a good thrashing!" And the more he thought of it the angrier he grew. He remembered also how his father said: "I see what a scoundrel you will turn out. I know you will. You are sure to become a cheat, if you go on like that." He had certainly forgotten how he felt when he was young! "What crime have I committed, I wonder? I wanted to go to the theatre, and having no money borrowed some from Petia Grouchetsky. Was that so very wicked of me? Another father would have been sorry for me; would have asked how it all happened; whereas he just called me names. He never thinks of anything but himself. When it is he who has not got something he wants—that is a different matter! Then all the house is upset by his shouts. And I—I am a scoundrel, a cheat, he says. No, I don't love him, although he is my father. It may be wrong, but I hate him."

There was a knock at the door. The servant brought a letter—a message from his friend. "They want an answer," said the servant.

The letter ran as follows: "I ask you now for the third time to pay me back the six roubles you have borrowed; you are trying to avoid me. That is not the way an honest man ought to behave. Will you please send the amount by my messenger? I am myself in a frightful fix. Can you not get the money somewhere?—Yours, according to whether you send the money or not, with scorn, or love, Grouchetsky."

"There we have it! Such a pig! Could he not wait a while? I will have another try."

Mitia went to his mother. This was his last hope. His mother was very kind, and hardly ever refused him anything. She would probably have helped him this time also out of his trouble, but she was in great anxiety: her younger child, Petia, a boy of two, had fallen ill. She got angry with Mitia for rushing so noisily into the nursery, and refused him almost without listening to what he had to say. Mitia muttered something to himself and turned to go. The mother felt sorry for him. "Wait, Mitia," she said; "I have not got the money you want now, but I will get it for you to-morrow."

But Mitia was still raging against his father.

"What is the use of having it to-morrow, when I want it to-day? I am going to see a friend. That is all I have got to say."

He went out, banging the door. . . .

"Nothing else is left to me. He will tell me how to pawn my watch," he thought, touching his watch in his pocket.

Mitia went to his room, took the coupon and the watch from the drawer, put on his coat, and went to Mahin.

II

Mahin was his schoolfellow, his senior, a grown-up young man with a moustache. He gambled, had a large feminine acquaintance, and always had ready cash. He lived with his aunt. Mitia quite realised that Mahin was not a respectable fellow, but when he was in his company he could not help doing what he wished. Mahin was in when Mitia called, and was just preparing to go to the theatre. His untidy room smelt of scented soap and eau-de-Cologne.

"That's awful, old chap," said Mahin, when Mitia telling him about his troubles, showed the coupon and the fifty kopeks, and added that he wanted nine roubles more. "We might, of course, go and pawn your watch. But we might do something far better." And Mahin winked an eye.

"What's that?"

"Something quite simple." Mahin took the coupon in his hand. "Put *one* before the 2.50 and it will be 12.50."

"But do such coupons exist?"

"Why, certainly; the thousand roubles notes have coupons of 12.50. I have cashed one in the same way."

"You don't say so?"

"Well, yes or no?" asked Mahin, taking the pen and smoothing the coupon with the fingers of his left hand.

"But it is wrong."

"Nonsense!"

"Nonsense, indeed," thought Mitia, and again his father's hard words came back to his memory. "Scoundrel! As you called me that, I might as well be it." He looked into Mahin's face. Mahin looked at him, smiling with perfect ease.

"Well?" he said.

"All right. I don't mind."

Mahin carefully wrote the unit in front of 2.50.

"Now let us go to the shop across the road; they sell photographers' materials there. I just happen to want a frame—for this young person here." He took out of his pocket a photograph of a young lady with large eyes, luxuriant hair, and an uncommonly well-developed bust.

"Is she not sweet? Eh?"

"Yes, yes . . . of course . . ."

"Well, you see.—But let us go."

Mahin took his coat, and they left the house.

III

The two boys, having rung the door-bell, entered the empty shop, which had shelves along the walls and photographic appliances on them, together with show-cases on the counters. A plain woman, with a kind face, came through the inner door and asked from behind the counter what they required.

"A nice frame, if you please, madam."

"At what price?" asked the woman; she wore mittens on her swollen fingers with which she rapidly handled picture-frames of different shapes.

"These are fifty kopeks each; and these are a little more expensive. There is rather a pretty one, of quite a new style; one rouble and twenty kopeks."

"All right, I will have this. But could not you make it cheaper? Let us say one rouble."

"We don't bargain in our shop," said the shopkeeper with a dignified air.

"Well, I will take it," said Mahin, and put the coupon on the counter. "Wrap up the frame and give me change. But please be quick. We must be off to the theatre, and it is getting late."

"You have plenty of time," said the shopkeeper, examining the coupon very closely because of her shortsightedness.

"It will look lovely in that frame, don't you think so?" said Mahin, turning to Mitia.

"Have you no small change?" asked the shop-woman.

"I am sorry, I have not. My father gave me that, so I have to cash it."

"But surely you have one rouble twenty?"

"I have only fifty kopeks in cash. But what are you afraid of? You don't think, I suppose, that we want to cheat you and give you bad money?"

"Oh, no; I don't mean anything of the sort."

"You had better give it to me back. We will cash it somewhere else."

"How much have I to pay you back? Eleven and something."

She made a calculation on the counter, opened the desk, took out a ten-roubles note, looked for change and added to the sum six twenty-kopeks coins and two five-kopek pieces.

"Please make a parcel of the frame," said Mahin, taking the money in a leisurely fashion.

"Yes, sir." She made a parcel and tied it with a string.

Mitia only breathed freely when the door bell rang behind them, and they were again in the street.

"There are ten roubles for you, and let me have the rest. I will give it back to you."

Mahin went off to the theatre, and Mitia called on Grouchetsky to repay the money he had borrowed from him.

IV

An hour after the boys were gone Eugene Mihailovich, the owner of the shop, came home, and began to count his receipts.

"Oh, you clumsy fool! Idiot that you are!" he shouted, addressing his wife, after having seen the coupon and noticed the forgery.

"But I have often seen you, Eugene, accepting coupons in payment, and precisely twelve rouble ones," retorted his wife, very humiliated, grieved, and all but bursting into tears. "I really don't know how they contrived to cheat me," she went on. "They were pupils of the school, in uniform. One of them was quite a handsome boy, and looked so comme il faut."

"A comme il faut fool, that is what you are!" The husband went on scolding her, while he counted the cash. . . . When I accept coupons, I see what is written on them. And you probably looked only at the boys' pretty faces. "You had better behave yourself in your old age."

His wife could not stand this, and got into a fury.

"That is just like you men! Blaming everybody around you. But when it is you who lose fifty-four roubles at cards—that is of no consequence in your eyes."

"That is a different matter

"I don't want to talk to you," said his wife, and went to her room. There she began to remind herself that her family was opposed to her marriage, thinking her present husband far below her in social rank, and that it was she who insisted on marrying him. Then she went on thinking of the child she had lost, and how indifferent her husband had been to their loss. She hated him so intensely at that moment that she wished for his death. Her wish frightened her, however, and she hurriedly began to dress and left the house. When her husband came from the shop to the inner rooms of their flat she was gone. Without waiting for him she had dressed and gone off to friends—a teacher of French in the school, a Russified Pole, and his wife— who had invited her and her husband to a party in their house that evening.

V

The guests at the party had tea and cakes offered to them, and sat down after that to play whist at a number of card-tables.

The partners of Eugene Mihailovich's wife were the host himself, an officer, and an old and very stupid lady in a wig, a widow who owned a music-shop; she loved playing cards and played remarkably well. But it was Eugene Mihailovich's wife who was the winner all the time. The best cards were continually in her hands. At her side she had a plate with grapes and a pear and was in the best of spirits.

"And Eugene Mihailovich? Why is he so late?" asked the hostess, who played at another table.

"Probably busy settling accounts," said Eugene Mihailovich's wife. "He has to pay off the tradesmen, to get in firewood." The quarrel she had with her husband revived in her memory; she frowned, and her hands, from which she had not taken off the mittens, shook with fury against him.

"Oh, there he is.—We have just been speaking of you," said the hostess to Eugene Mihailovich, who came in at that very moment. "Why are you so late?"

"I was busy," answered Eugene Mihailovich, in a gay voice, rubbing his hands. And to his wife's surprise he came to her side and said,—"You know, I managed to get rid of the coupon."

"No! You don't say so!"

"Yes, I used it to pay for a cartload of firewood I bought from a peasant."

And Eugene Mihailovich related with great indignation to the company present—his wife adding more details to his narrative—how his wife had been cheated by two unscrupulous schoolboys.

"Well, and now let us sit down to work," he said, taking his place at one of the whist-tables when his turn came, and beginning to shuffle the cards.

VI

Eugene Mihailovich had actually used the coupon to buy firewood from the peasant Ivan Mironov, who had thought of setting up in business on the seventeen roubles he possessed. He hoped in this way to earn another eight roubles, and with the twenty-five roubles thus amassed he intended to buy a good strong horse, which he would want in the spring for work in the fields and for driving on the roads, as his old horse was almost played out.

Ivan Mironov's commercial method consisted in buying from the stores a cord of wood and dividing it into five cartloads, and then driving about the town, selling each of these at the price the stores charged for a quarter of a cord. That unfortunate day Ivan Mironov drove out very early with half a cartload, which he soon sold. He loaded up again with another cartload which he hoped to sell, but he looked in vain for a customer; no one would buy it. It was his bad luck all that day to come across experienced towns-people, who knew all the tricks of the peasants in selling firewood, and would not believe that he had actually brought the wood from the country as he assured them. He got hungry, and felt cold in his ragged woollen coat. It was nearly below zero when evening came on; his horse which he had treated without mercy, hoping soon to sell it to the knacker's yard, refused to move a step. So Ivan Mironov was quite ready to sell his firewood at a loss when he met Eugene Mihailovich, who was on his way home from the tobacconist.

"Buy my cartload of firewood, sir. I will give it to you cheap. My poor horse is tired, and can't go any farther."

"Where do you come from?"

"From the country, sir. This firewood is from our place. Good dry wood, I can assure you."

"Good wood indeed! I know your tricks. Well, what is your price?"

Ivan Mironov began by asking a high price, but reduced it once, and finished by selling the cartload for just what it had cost him.

"I'm giving it to you cheap, just to please you, sir.—Besides, I am glad it is not a long way to your house," he added.

Eugene Mihailovich did not bargain very much. He did not mind paying a little more, because he was delighted to think he could make use of the coupon and get rid of it. With great difficulty Ivan Mironov managed at last, by pulling the shafts himself, to drag his cart into the courtyard, where he was obliged to unload the firewood unaided and pile it up in the shed. The yard-porter was out. Ivan Mironov hesitated at first to accept the coupon, but Eugene Mihailovich insisted, and as he looked a very important person the peasant at last agreed.

He went by the backstairs to the servants' room, crossed himself before the ikon, wiped his beard which was covered with icicles, turned up the skirts of his coat, took out of his pocket a leather purse, and out of the purse eight roubles and fifty kopeks, and handed the change to Eugene Mihailovich. Carefully folding the coupon, he put it in the purse. Then, according to custom, he thanked the gentleman for his kindness, and, using the whip-handle instead of the lash, he belaboured the half-frozen horse that he had doomed to an early death, and betook himself to a public-house.

Arriving there, Ivan Mironov called for vodka and tea for which he paid eight kopeks. Comfortable and warm after the tea, he chatted in the very best of spirits with a yard-porter who was sitting at his table. Soon he grew communicative and told his companion all about the conditions of his life. He told him he came from the village Vassilievsky, twelve miles from town, and also that he had his allotment of land given to him by his family, as he wanted to live apart from his father and his brothers; that he had a wife and two children; the elder boy went to school, and did not yet help him in his work. He also said he lived in lodgings and intended going to the horse-fair the next day to look for a good horse, and, may be, to buy one. He went on to state that he had now nearly twenty-five roubles—only one rouble short—and that half of it was a coupon. He took the coupon out of his purse to show to his new friend. The yard-porter was an illiterate man, but he said he had had such coupons given him by lodgers to change; that they were good; but that one might also chance on forged ones; so he advised the peasant, for the sake of security, to change it at once at the counter. Ivan Mironov gave the coupon to the waiter and asked for change. The waiter, however, did not bring the change, but came back with the manager, a bald-headed man with a shining face, who was holding the coupon in his fat hand.

"Your money is no good," he said, showing the coupon, but apparently determined not to give it back.

"The coupon must be all right. I got it from a gentleman."

"It is bad, I tell you. The coupon is forged."

"Forged? Give it back to me."

"I will not. You fellows have got to be punished for such tricks. Of course, you did it yourself—you and some of your rascally friends."

"Give me the money. What right have you—"

"Sidor! Call a policeman," said the barman to the waiter. Ivan Mironov was rather drunk, and in that condition was hard to manage. He seized the manager by the collar and began to shout.

"Give me back my money, I say. I will go to the gentleman who gave it to me. I know where he lives."

The manager had to struggle with all his force to get loose from Ivan Mironov, and his shirt was torn,—"Oh, that's the way you behave! Get hold of him."

The waiter took hold of Ivan Mironov; at that moment the policeman arrived. Looking very important, he inquired what had happened, and unhesitatingly gave his orders:

"Take him to the police-station."

As to the coupon, the policeman put it in his pocket; Ivan Mironov, together with his horse, was brought to the nearest station.

VII

Ivan Mironov had to spend the night in the police-station, in the company of drunkards and thieves. It was noon of the next day when he was summoned to the police officer; put through a close examination, and sent in the care of a policeman to Eugene Mihailovich's shop. Ivan Mironov remembered the street and the house.

The policeman asked for the shopkeeper, showed him the coupon and confronted him with Ivan Mironov, who declared that he had received the coupon in that very place. Eugene Mihailovich at once assumed a very severe and astonished air.

"You are mad, my good fellow," he said. "I have never seen this man before in my life," he added, addressing the policeman.

"It is a sin, sir," said Ivan Mironov. "Think of the hour when you will die."

"Why, you must be dreaming! You have sold your firewood to some one else," said Eugene Mihailovich. "But wait a minute. I will go and ask my wife whether she bought any firewood yesterday." Eugene Mihailovich left them and immediately called the yard-porter Vassily, a strong, handsome, quick, cheerful, well-dressed man.

He told Vassily that if any one should inquire where the last supply of firewood was bought, he was to say they'd got it from the stores, and not from a peasant in the street.

"A peasant has come," he said to Vassily, "who has declared to the police that I gave him a forged coupon. He is a fool and talks nonsense, but you, are a clever man. Mind you say that we always get the firewood from the stores. And, by the way, I've been thinking some time of giving you money to buy a new jacket," added Eugene Mihailovich, and gave the man five roubles. Vassily looking with pleasure first at the five rouble note, then at Eugene Mihailovich's face, shook his head and smiled.

"I know, those peasant folks have no brains. Ignorance, of course. Don't you be uneasy. I know what I have to say."

Ivan Mironov, with tears in his eyes, implored Eugene Mihailovich over and over again to acknowledge the coupon he had given him, and the yard-porter to believe what he said, but it proved quite useless; they both insisted that they had never bought firewood from a peasant in the street. The policeman brought Ivan Mironov back to the police-station, and he was charged with forging the coupon. Only after taking the advice of a drunken office clerk in the same cell with him, and bribing the police officer with five roubles, did Ivan Mironov get out of jail, without the coupon, and with only seven roubles left out of the twenty-five he had the day before.

Of these seven roubles he spent three in the public-house and came home to his wife dead drunk, with a bruised and swollen face.

His wife was expecting a child, and felt very ill. She began to scold her husband; he pushed her away, and she struck him. Without answering a word he lay down on the plank and began to weep bitterly.

Not till the next day did he tell his wife what had actually happened. She believed him at once, and thoroughly cursed the dastardly rich man who had cheated Ivan. He was sobered now, and remembering the advice a workman had given him, with whom he had many a drink the day before, decided to go to a lawyer and tell him of the wrong the owner of the photograph shop had done him.

VIII

The lawyer consented to take proceedings on behalf of Ivan Mironov, not so much for the sake of the fee, as because he believed the peasant, and was revolted by the wrong done to him.

Both parties appeared in the court when the case was tried, and the yard-porter Vassily was summoned as witness. They repeated in the court all they had said before to the police officials. Ivan Mironov again called to his aid the name of the Divinity, and reminded the shopkeeper of the hour of death. Eugene Mihailovich, although quite aware of his wickedness, and the risks he was running, despite the rebukes of his conscience, could not now change his testimony, and went on calmly to deny all the allegations made against him.

The yard-porter Vassily had received another ten roubles from his master, and, quite unperturbed, asserted with a smile that he did not know anything about Ivan Mironov. And when he was called upon to take the oath, he overcame his inner qualms, and repeated with assumed ease the terms of the oath, read to him by the old priest appointed to the court. By the holy Cross and the Gospel, he swore that he spoke the whole truth.

The case was decided against Ivan Mironov, who was sentenced to pay five roubles for expenses. This sum Eugene Mihailovich generously paid for him. Before dismissing Ivan Mironov, the judge severely admonished him, saying he ought to take care in the future not to accuse respectable people, and that he also ought to be thankful that he was not forced to pay the costs, and that he had escaped a prosecution for slander, for which he would have been condemned to three months' imprisonment.

"I offer my humble thanks," said Ivan Mironov; and, shaking his head, left the court with a heavy sigh.

The whole thing seemed to have ended well for Eugene Mihailovich and the yard-porter Vassily. But only in appearance. Something had happened which was not noticed by any one, but which was much more important than all that had been exposed to view.

Vassily had left his village and settled in town over two years ago. As time went on he sent less and less money to his father, and he did not ask his wife, who remained at home, to join him. He was in no need of her; he could in town have as many wives as he wished, and much better ones too than that clumsy, village-bred woman. Vassily, with each recurring year, became more and more familiar with the ways of the town people, forgetting the conventions of a country life. There everything was so vulgar, so grey, so poor and untidy. Here, in town, all seemed on the contrary so refined, nice, clean, and rich; so orderly too. And he became more and more convinced that people in the country live just like wild beasts, having no idea of what life is, and that only life in town is real. He read books written by clever writers, and went to the performances in the Peoples' Palace. In the country, people would not see such wonders even in dreams. In the country old men say: "Obey the law, and live with your wife; work; don't eat too much; don't care for finery," while here, in town, all the clever and learned people—those, of course, who know what in reality the law is—only pursue their own pleasures. And they are the better for it.

Previous to the incident of the forged coupon, Vassily could not actually believe that rich people lived without any moral law. But after that, still more after having perjured himself, and not being the worse for it in spite of his fears—on the contrary, he had gained ten roubles out of it—Vassily became firmly convinced that no moral laws whatever exist, and that the only thing to do is to pursue one's own interests and pleasures. This he now made his rule in life. He accordingly got as much profit as he could out of purchasing goods for lodgers. But this did not pay all his expenses. Then he took to stealing, whenever chance offered—money and all sorts of valuables. One day he stole a purse full of money from Eugene Mihailovich, but was found out. Eugene Mihailovich did not hand him over to the police, but dismissed him on the spot.

Vassily had no wish whatever to return home to his village, and remained in Moscow with his sweetheart, looking out for a new job. He got one as yard-porter at a grocer's, but with only small wages. The next day after he had entered that service he was caught stealing bags. The grocer did not call in the police, but gave him a good thrashing and turned him out. After that he could not find work. The money he had left was soon gone; he had to sell all his clothes and went about nearly in rags. His sweetheart left him. But notwithstanding, he kept up his high spirits, and when the spring came he started to walk home.

IX

Peter Nikolaevich Sventizky, a short man in black spectacles (he had weak eyes, and was threatened with complete blindness), got up, as was his custom, at dawn of day, had a cup of tea, and putting on his short fur coat trimmed with astrachan, went to look after the work on his estate.

Peter Nikolaevich had been an official in the Customs, and had gained eighteen thousand roubles during his service. About twelve years ago he quitted the service—not quite of his own accord: as a matter of fact he had been compelled to leave—and bought an estate from a young landowner who had dissipated his fortune. Peter Nikolaevich had married at an earlier period, while still an official in the Customs. His wife, who belonged to an old noble family, was an orphan, and was left without money. She was a tall, stoutish, good-looking woman. They had no children. Peter Nikolaevich had considerable practical talents and a strong will. He was the son of a Polish gentleman, and knew nothing about agriculture and land management; but when he acquired an estate of his own, he managed it so well that after fifteen years the waste piece of land, consisting of three hundred acres, became a model estate. All the buildings, from the dwelling-house to the corn stores and the shed for the fire engine were solidly built, had iron roofs, and were painted at the right time. In the tool house carts, ploughs, harrows, stood in perfect order, the harness was well cleaned and oiled. The horses were not very big, but all home-bred, grey, well fed, strong and devoid of blemish.

The threshing machine worked in a roofed barn, the forage was kept in a separate shed, and a paved drain was made from the stables. The cows were home-bred, not very large, but giving plenty of milk; fowls were also kept in the poultry yard, and the hens were of a special kind, laying a great quantity of eggs. In the orchard the fruit trees were well whitewashed and propped on poles to enable them to grow straight. Everything was looked after—solid, clean, and in perfect order. Peter Nikolaevich rejoiced in the perfect condition of his estate, and was proud to have achieved it—not by oppressing the peasants, but, on the contrary, by the extreme fairness of his dealings with them.

Among the nobles of his province he belonged to the advanced party, and was more inclined to liberal than conservative views, always taking the side of the peasants against those who were still in favour of serfdom. "Treat them well, and they will be fair to you," he used to say. Of course, he did not overlook any carelessness on the part of those who worked on his estate, and he urged them on to work if they were lazy; but then he gave them good lodging, with plenty of good food, paid their wages without any delay, and gave them drinks on days of festival.

Walking cautiously on the melting snow—for the time of the year was February—Peter Nikolaevich passed the stables, and made his way to the cottage where his workmen were lodged. It was still dark, the darker because of the dense fog; but the windows of the cottage were lighted. The men had already got up. His intention was to urge them to begin work. He had arranged that they should drive out to the forest and bring back the last supply of firewood he needed before spring.

"What is that?" he thought, seeing the door of the stable wide open. "Hallo, who is there?"

No answer. Peter Nikolaevich stepped into the stable. It was dark; the ground was soft under his feet, and the air smelt of dung; on the right side of the door were two loose boxes for a pair of grey horses. Peter Nikolaevich stretched out his hand in their direction—one box was empty. He put out his foot—the horse might have been lying down. But his foot did not touch anything solid. "Where could they have taken the horse?" he thought. They certainly had not harnessed it; all the sledges stood still outside. Peter Nikolaevich went out of the stable.

"Stepan, come here!" he called.

Stepan was the head of the workmen's gang. He was just stepping out of the cottage.

"Here I am!" he said, in a cheerful voice. "Oh, is that you, Peter Nikolaevich? Our men are coming."

"Why is the stable door open?

"Is it? I don't know anything about it. I say, Proshka, bring the lantern!"

Proshka came with the lantern. They all went to the stable, and Stepan knew at once what had happened.

"Thieves have been here, Peter Nikolaevich," he said. "The lock is broken."

"No; you don't say so!"

"Yes, the brigands! I don't see 'Mashka.' 'Hawk' is here. But 'Beauty' is not. Nor yet 'Dapple-grey.'"

Three horses had been stolen!

Peter Nikolaevich did not utter a word at first. He only frowned and took deep breaths.

"Oh," he said after a while. "If only I could lay hands on them! Who was on guard?"

"Peter. He evidently fell asleep."

Peter Nikolaevich called in the police, and making an appeal to all the authorities, sent his men to track the thieves. But the horses were not to be found.

"Wicked people," said Peter Nikolaevich. "How could they! I was always so kind to them. Now, wait! Brigands! Brigands the whole lot of them. I will no longer be kind."

X

In the meanwhile the horses, the grey ones, had all been disposed of; Mashka was sold to the gipsies for eighteen roubles; Dapple-grey was exchanged for another horse, and passed over to another peasant who lived forty miles away from the estate; and Beauty died on the way.

The man who conducted the whole affair was—Ivan Mironov. He had been employed on the estate, and knew all the whereabouts of Peter Nikolaevich. He wanted to get back the money he had lost, and stole the horses for that reason.

After his misfortune with the forged coupon, Ivan Mironov took to drink; and all he possessed would have gone on drink if it had not been for his wife, who locked up his clothes, the horses' collars, and all the rest of what he would otherwise have squandered in public-houses. In his drunken state Ivan Mironov was continually thinking, not only of the man who had wronged him, but of all the rich people who live on robbing the poor. One day he had a drink with some peasants from the suburbs of Podolsk, and was walking home together with them. On the way the peasants, who were completely drunk, told him they had stolen a horse from a peasant's cottage. Ivan Mironov got angry, and began to abuse the horse-thieves.

"What a shame!" he said. "A horse is like a brother to the peasant. And you robbed him of it? It is a great sin, I tell you. If you go in for stealing horses, steal them from the landowners. They are worse than dogs, and deserve anything."

The talk went on, and the peasants from Podolsk told him that it required a great deal of cunning to steal a horse on an estate.

"You must know all the ins and outs of the place, and must have somebody on the spot to help you."

Then it occurred to Ivan Mironov that he knew a landowner—Sventizky; he had worked on his estate, and Sventizky, when paying him off, had deducted one rouble and a half for a broken tool. He remembered well the grey horses which he used to drive at Sventizky's.

Ivan Mironov called on Peter Nikolaevich pretending to ask for employment, but really in order to get the information he wanted. He took precautions to make sure that the watchman was absent, and that the horses were standing in their boxes in the stable. He brought the thieves to the place, and helped them to carry off the three horses.

They divided their gains, and Ivan Mironov returned to his wife with five roubles in his pocket. He had nothing to do at home, having no horse to work in the field, and therefore continued to steal horses in company with professional horse-thieves and gipsies.

XI

Peter Nikolaevich Sventizky did his best to discover who had stolen his horses. He knew somebody on the estate must have helped the thieves, and began to suspect all his staff. He inquired who had slept out that night, and the gang of the working men told him Proshka had not been in the whole night. Proshka, or Prokofy Nikolaevich, was a young fellow who had just finished his military service, handsome, and skilful in all he did; Peter Nikolaevich employed him at times as coachman. The district constable was a friend of Peter Nikolaevich, as were the provincial head of the police, the marshal of the nobility, and also the rural councillor and the examining magistrate. They all came to his house on his saint's day, drinking the cherry brandy he offered them with pleasure, and eating the nice preserved mushrooms of all kinds to accompany the liqueurs. They all sympathised with him in his trouble and tried to help him.

"You always used to take the side of the peasants," said the district constable, "and there you are! I was right in saying they are worse than wild beasts. Flogging is the only way to keep them in order. Well, you say it is all Proshka's doings. Is it not he who was your coachman sometimes?"

"Yes, that is he."

"Will you kindly call him?"

Proshka was summoned before the constable, who began to examine him.

"Where were you that night?"

Proshka pushed back his hair, and his eyes sparkled.

"At home."

"How so? All the men say you were not in."

"Just as you please, your honour."

"My pleasure has nothing to do with the matter. Tell me where you were that night."

"At home."

"Very well. Policeman, bring him to the police-station."

The reason why Proshka did not say where he had been that night was that he had spent it with his sweetheart, Parasha, and had promised not to give her away. He kept his word. No proofs were discovered against him, and he was soon discharged. But Peter Nikolaevich was convinced that Prokofy had been at the bottom of the whole affair, and began to hate him. One day Proshka bought as usual at the merchant's two measures of oats. One and a half he gave to the horses, and half a measure he gave back to the merchant; the money for it he spent in drink. Peter Nikolaevich found it out, and charged Prokofy with cheating. The judge sentenced the man to three months' imprisonment.

Prokofy had a rather proud nature, and thought himself superior to others. Prison was a great humiliation for him. He came out of it very depressed; there was nothing more to be proud of in life. And more than that, he felt extremely bitter, not only against Peter Nikolaevich, but against the whole world.

On the whole, as all the people around him noticed, Prokofy became another man after his imprisonment, both careless and lazy; he took to drink, and he was soon caught stealing clothes at some woman's house, and found himself again in prison.

All that Peter Nikolaevich discovered about his grey horses was the hide of one of them, Beauty, which had been found somewhere on the estate. The fact that the thieves had got off scot-free irritated Peter Nikolaevich still more. He was unable now to speak of the peasants or to look at them without anger. And whenever he could he tried to oppress them.

XII

After having got rid of the coupon, Eugene Mihailovich forgot all about it; but his wife, Maria Vassilievna, could not forgive herself for having been taken in, nor yet her husband for his cruel words. And most of all she was furious against the two boys who had so skilfully cheated her. From the day she had accepted the forged coupon as payment, she looked closely at all the schoolboys who came in her way in the streets. One day she met Mahin, but did not recognise him, for on seeing her he made a face which quite changed his features. But when, a fortnight after the incident with the coupon, she met Mitia Smokovnikov face to face, she knew him at once.

She let him pass her, then turned back and followed him, and arriving at his house she made inquiries as to whose son he was. The next day she went to the school and met the divinity instructor, the priest Michael Vedensky, in the hall. He asked her what she wanted. She answered that she wished to see the head of the school. "He is not quite well," said the priest. "Can I be of any use to you, or give him your message?"

Maria Vassilievna thought that she might as well tell the priest what was the matter. Michael Vedensky was a widower, and a very ambitious man. A year ago he had met Mitia Smokovnikov's father in society, and had had a discussion with him on religion. Smokovnikov had beaten him decisively on all points; indeed, he had made him appear quite ridiculous. Since that time the priest had decided to pay special attention to Smokovnikov's son; and, finding him as indifferent to religious matters as his father was, he began to persecute him, and even brought about his failure in examinations.

When Maria Vassilievna told him what young Smokovnikov had done to her, Vedensky could not help feeling an inner satisfaction. He saw in the boy's conduct a proof of the utter wickedness of those who are not guided by the rules of the Church. He decided to take advantage of this great opportunity of warning unbelievers of the perils that threatened them. At all events, he wanted to persuade himself that this was the only motive that guided him in the course he had resolved to take. But at the bottom of his heart he was only anxious to get his revenge on the proud atheist.

"Yes, it is very sad indeed," said Father Michael, toying with the cross he was wearing over his priestly robes, and passing his hands over its polished sides. "I am very glad you have given me your confidence. As a servant of the Church I shall admonish the young man—of course with the utmost kindness. I shall certainly do it in the way that befits my holy office," said Father Michael to himself, really thinking that he had forgotten the ill-feeling the boy's father had towards him. He firmly believed the boy's soul to be the only object of his pious care.

The next day, during the divinity lesson which Father Michael was giving to Mitia Smokovnikov's class, he narrated the incident of the forged coupon, adding that the culprit had been one of the pupils of the school. "It was a very wicked thing to do," he said; "but to deny the crime is still worse. If it is true that the sin has been committed by one of you, let the guilty one confess." In saying this, Father Michael looked sharply at Mitia Smokovnikov. All the boys, following his glance, turned also to Mitia, who blushed, and felt extremely ill at ease, with large beads of perspiration on his face. Finally, he burst into tears, and ran out of the classroom. His mother, noticing his trouble, found out the truth, ran at once to the photographer's shop, paid over the twelve roubles and fifty kopeks to Maria Vassilievna, and made her promise to deny the boy's guilt. She further implored Mitia to hide the truth from everybody, and in any case to withhold it from his father.

Accordingly, when Fedor Mihailovich had heard of the incident in the divinity class, and his son, questioned by him, had denied all accusations, he called at once on the head of the school, told him what had happened, expressed his indignation at Father Michael's conduct, and said he would not let matters remain as they were.

Father Michael was sent for, and immediately fell into a hot dispute with Smokovnikov.

"A stupid woman first falsely accused my son, then retracts her accusation, and you of course could not hit on anything more sensible to do than to slander an honest and truthful boy!"

"I did not slander him, and I must beg you not to address me in such a way. You forget what is due to my cloth."

"Your cloth is of no consequence to me."

"Your perversity in matters of religion is known to everybody in the town!" replied Father Michael; and he was so transported with anger that his long thin head quivered.

"Gentlemen! Father Michael!" exclaimed the director of the school, trying to appease their wrath. But they did not listen to him.

"It is my duty as a priest to look after the religious and moral education of our pupils."

"Oh, cease your pretence to be religious! Oh, stop all this humbug of religion! As if I did not know that you believe neither in God nor Devil."

"I consider it beneath my dignity to talk to a man like you," said Father Michael, very much hurt by Smokovnikov's last words, the more so because he knew they were true.

Michael Vedensky carried on his studies in the academy for priests, and that is why, for a long time past, he ceased to believe in what he confessed to be his creed and in what he preached from the pulpit; he only knew that men ought to force themselves to believe in what he tried to make himself believe.

Smokovnikov was not shocked by Father Michael's conduct; he only thought it illustrative of the influence the Church was beginning to exercise on society, and he told all his friends how his son had been insulted by the priest.

Seeing not only young minds, but also the elder generation, contaminated by atheistic tendencies, Father Michael became more and more convinced of the necessity of fighting those tendencies. The more he condemned the unbelief of Smokovnikov, and those like him, the more confident he grew in the firmness of his own faith, and the less he felt the need of making sure of it, or of bringing his life into harmony with it. His faith, acknowledged as such by all the world around him, became Father Michael's very best weapon with which to fight those who denied it.

The thoughts aroused in him by his conflict with Smokovnikov, together with the annoyance of being blamed by his chiefs in the school, made him carry out the purpose he had entertained ever since his wife's death—of taking monastic orders, and of following the course carried out by some of his fellow-pupils in the academy. One of them was already a bishop, another an archimandrite and on the way to become a bishop.

At the end of the term Michael Vedensky gave up his post in the school, took orders under the name of Missael, and very soon got a post as rector in a seminary in a town on the river Volga.

XIII

Meanwhile the yard-porter Vassily was marching on the open road down to the south.

He walked in daytime, and when night came some policeman would get him shelter in a peasant's cottage. He was given bread everywhere, and sometimes he was asked to sit down to the evening meal. In a village in the Orel district, where he had stayed for the night, he heard that a merchant who had hired the landowner's orchard for the season, was looking out for strong and able men to serve as watchmen for the fruit-crops. Vassily was tired of tramping, and as he had also no desire whatever to go back to his native village, he went to the man who owned the orchard, and got engaged as watchman for five roubles a month.

Vassily found it very agreeable to live in his orchard shed, and all the more so when the apples and pears began to grow ripe, and when the men from the barn supplied him every day with large bundles of fresh straw from the threshing machine. He used to lie the whole day long on the fragrant straw, with fresh, delicately smelling apples in heaps at his side, looking out in every direction to prevent the village boys from stealing fruit; and he used to whistle and sing meanwhile, to amuse himself. He knew no end of songs, and had a fine voice. When peasant women and young girls came to ask for apples, and to have a chat with him, Vassily gave them larger or smaller apples according as he liked their looks, and received eggs or money in return.

The rest of the time he had nothing to do, but to lie on his back and get up for his meals in the kitchen. He had only one shirt left, one of pink cotton, and that was in holes. But he was strongly built and enjoyed excellent health. When the kettle with black gruel was taken from the stove and served to the working men, Vassily used to eat enough for three, and filled the old watchman on the estate with unceasing wonder. At nights Vassily never slept. He whistled or shouted from time to time to keep off thieves, and his piercing, cat-like eyes saw clearly in the darkness.

One night a company of young lads from the village made their way stealthily to the orchard to shake down apples from the trees. Vassily, coming noiselessly from behind, attacked them; they tried to escape, but he took one of them prisoner to his master.

Vassily's first shed stood at the farthest end of the orchard, but after the pears had been picked he had to remove to another shed only forty paces away from the house of his master. He liked this new place very much. The whole day long he could see the young ladies and gentlemen enjoying themselves; going out for drives in the evenings and quite late at nights, playing the piano or the violin, and singing and dancing. He saw the ladies sitting with the young students on the window sills, engaged in animated conversation, and then going in pairs to walk the dark avenue of lime trees, lit up only by streaks of moonlight. He saw the servants running about with food and drink, he saw the cooks, the stewards, the laundresses, the gardeners, the coachmen, hard at work to supply their masters with food and drink and constant amusement. Sometimes the young people from the master's house came to the shed, and Vassily offered them the choicest apples, juicy and red. The young ladies used to take large bites out of the apples on the spot, praising their taste, and spoke French to one another—Vassily quite understood it was all about him—and asked Vassily to sing for them.

Vassily felt the greatest admiration for his master's mode of living, which reminded him of what he had seen in Moscow; and he became more and more convinced that the only thing that mattered in life was money. He thought and thought how to get hold of a large sum of money. He remembered his former ways of making small profits whenever he could, and came to the conclusion that that was altogether wrong. Occasional stealing is of no use, he thought. He must arrange a well-prepared plan, and after getting all the information he wanted, carry out his purpose so as to avoid detection.

After the feast of Nativity of the Blessed Virgin Mary, the last crop of autumn apples was gathered; the master was content with the results, paid off Vassily, and gave him an extra sum as reward for his faithful service.

Vassily put on his new jacket, and a new hat—both were presents from his master's son—but did not make his way homewards. He hated the very thought of the vulgar peasants' life. He went back to Moscow in company of some drunken soldiers, who had been watchmen in the orchard together with him. On his arrival there he at once resolved, under cover of night, to break into the shop where he had been employed, and beaten, and then turned out by the proprietor without being paid. He knew the place well, and knew where the money was locked up. So he bade the soldiers, who helped him, keep watch outside, and forcing the courtyard door entered the shop and took all the money he could lay his hands on. All this was done very cleverly, and no trace was left of the burglary. The money Vassily had found in the shop amounted to 370 roubles. He gave a hundred roubles to his assistants, and with the rest left for another town where he gave way to dissipation in company of friends of both sexes. The police traced his movements, and when at last he was arrested and put into prison he had hardly anything left out of the money which he had stolen.

XIV

Ivan Mironov had become a very clever, fearless and successful horse-thief. Afimia, his wife, who at first used to abuse him for his evil ways, as she called it, was now quite content and felt proud of her husband, who possessed a new sheepskin coat, while she also had a warm jacket and a new fur cloak.

In the village and throughout the whole district every one knew quite well that Ivan Mironov was at the bottom of all the horse-stealing; but nobody would give him away, being afraid of the consequences. Whenever suspicion fell on him, he managed to clear his character. Once during the night he stole horses from the pasture ground in the village Kolotovka. He generally preferred to steal horses from landowners or tradespeople. But this was a harder job, and when he had no chance of success he did not mind robbing peasants too. In Kolotovka he drove off the horses without making sure whose they were. He did not go himself to the spot, but sent a young and clever fellow, Gerassim, to do the stealing for him. The peasants only got to know of the theft at dawn; they rushed in all directions to hunt for the robbers. The horses, meanwhile, were hidden in a ravine in the forest lands belonging to the state.

Ivan Mironov intended to leave them there till the following night, and then to transport them with the utmost haste a hundred miles away to a man he knew. He visited Gerassim in the forest, to see how he was getting on, brought him a pie and some vodka, and was returning home by a side track in the forest where he hoped to meet nobody. But by ill-luck, he chanced on the keeper of the forest, a retired soldier.

"I say! Have you been looking for mushrooms?" asked the soldier.

"There were none to be found," answered Ivan Mironov, showing the basket of lime bark he had taken with him in case he might want it.

"Yes, mushrooms are scarce this summer," said the soldier. He stood still for a moment, pondered, and then went his way. He clearly saw that something was wrong. Ivan Mironov had no business whatever to take early morning walks in that forest. The soldier went back after a while and looked round. Suddenly he heard the snorting of horses in the ravine. He made his way cautiously to the place whence the sounds came. The grass in the ravine was trodden down, and the marks of horses' hoofs were clearly to be seen. A little further he saw Gerassim, who was sitting and eating his meal, and the horses tied to a tree.

The soldier ran to the village and brought back the bailiff, a police officer, and two witnesses. They surrounded on three sides the spot where Gerassim was sitting and seized the man. He did not deny anything; but, being drunk, told them at once how Ivan Mironov had given him plenty of drink, and induced him to steal the horses; he also said that Ivan Mironov had promised to come that night in order to take the horses away. The peasants left the horses and Gerassim in the ravine, and hiding behind the trees prepared to lie in ambush for Ivan Mironov. When it grew dark, they heard a whistle. Gerassim answered it with a similar sound. The moment Ivan Mironov descended the slope, the peasants surrounded him and brought him back to the village. The next morning a crowd assembled in front of the bailiff's cottage. Ivan Mironov was brought out and subjected to a close examination. Stepan Pelageushkine, a tall, stooping man with long arms, an aquiline nose, and a gloomy face was the first to put questions to him. Stepan had terminated his military service, and was of a solitary turn of mind. When he had separated from his father, and started his own home, he had his first experience of losing a horse. After that he worked for two years in the mines, and made money enough to buy two horses. These two had been stolen by Ivan Mironov.

"Tell me where my horses are!" shouted Stepan, pale with fury, alternately looking at the ground and at Ivan Mironov's face.

Ivan Mironov denied his guilt. Then Stepan aimed so violent a blow at his face that he smashed his nose and the blood spurted out.

"Tell the truth, I say, or I'll kill you!"

Ivan Mironov kept silent, trying to avoid the blows by stooping. Stepan hit him twice more with his long arm. Ivan Mironov remained silent, turning his head backwards and forwards.

"Beat him, all of you!" cried the bailiff, and the whole crowd rushed upon Ivan Mironov. He fell without a word to the ground, and then shouted,—"Devils, wild beasts, kill me if that's what you want! I am not afraid of you!"

Stepan seized a stone out of those that had been collected for the purpose, and with a heavy blow smashed Ivan Mironov's head.

XV

Ivan Mironov's murderers were brought to trial, Stepan Pelageushkine among them. He had a heavier charge to answer than the others, all the witnesses having stated that it was he who had smashed Ivan Mironov's head with a stone. Stepan concealed nothing when in court. He contented himself with explaining that, having been robbed of his two last horses, he had informed the police. Now it was comparatively easy at that time to trace the horses with the help of professional thieves among the gipsies. But the police officer would not even permit him, and no search had been ordered.

"Nothing else could be done with such a man. He has ruined us all."

"But why did not the others attack him. It was you alone who broke his head open."

"That is false. We all fell upon him. The village agreed to kill him. I only gave the final stroke. What is the use of inflicting unnecessary sufferings on a man?"

The judges were astonished at Stepan's wonderful coolness in narrating the story of his crime—how the peasants fell upon Ivan Mironov, and how he had given the final stroke. Stepan actually did not see anything particularly revolting in this murder. During his military service he had been ordered on one occasion to shoot a soldier, and, now with regard to Ivan Mironov, he saw nothing loathsome in it. "A man shot is a dead man—that's all. It was him to-day, it might be me to-morrow," he thought. Stepan was only sentenced to one year's imprisonment, which was a mild punishment for what he had done. His peasant's dress was taken away from him and put in the prison stores, and he had a prison suit and felt boots given to him instead. Stepan had never had much respect for the authorities, but now he became quite convinced that all the chiefs, all the fine folk, all except the Czar—who alone had pity on the peasants and was just—all were robbers who suck blood out of the people. All he heard from the deported convicts, and those sentenced to hard labour, with whom he had made friends in prisons, confirmed him in his views. One man had been sentenced to hard labour for having convicted his superiors of a theft; another for having struck an official who had unjustly confiscated the property of a peasant; a third because he forged bank notes. The well-to-do-people, the merchants, might do whatever they chose and come to no harm; but a poor peasant, for a trumpery reason or for none at all, was sent to prison to become food for vermin.

He had visits from his wife while in prison. Her life without him was miserable enough, when, to make it worse, her cottage was destroyed by fire. She was completely ruined, and had to take to begging with her children. His wife's misery embittered Stepan still more. He got on very badly with all the people in the prison; was rude to every one; and one day he nearly killed the cook with an axe, and therefore got an additional year in prison. In the course of that year he received the news that his wife was dead, and that he had no longer a home.

When Stepan had finished his time in prison, he was taken to the prison stores, and his own dress was taken down from the shelf and handed to him.

"Where am I to go now?" he asked the prison officer, putting on his old dress.

"Why, home."

"I have no home. I shall have to go on the road. Robbery will not be a pleasant occupation."

"In that case you will soon be back here."

"I am not so sure of that."

And Stepan left the prison. Nevertheless he took the road to his own place. He had nowhere else to turn.

On his way he stopped for a night's rest in an inn that had a public bar attached to it. The inn was kept by a fat man from the town, Vladimir, and he knew Stepan. He knew that Stepan had been put into prison through ill luck, and did not mind giving him shelter for the night. He was a rich man, and had persuaded his neighbour's wife to leave her husband and come to live with him. She lived in his house as his wife, and helped him in his business as well.

Stepan knew all about the innkeeper's affairs—how he had wronged the peasant, and how the woman who was living with him had left her husband. He saw her now sitting at the table in a rich dress, and looking very hot as she drank her tea. With great condescension she asked Stepan to have tea with her. No other travellers were stopping in the inn that night. Stepan was given a place in the kitchen where he might sleep. Matrena—that was the woman's name—cleared the table and went to her room. Stepan went to lie down on the large stove in the kitchen, but he could not sleep, and the wood splinters put on the stove to dry were crackling under him, as he tossed from side to side. He could not help thinking of his host's fat paunch protruding under the belt of his shirt, which had lost its colour from having been washed ever so many times. Would not it be a good thing to make a good clean incision in that paunch. And that woman, too, he thought.

One moment he would say to himself, "I had better go from here tomorrow, bother them all!" But then again Ivan Mironov came back to his mind, and he went on thinking of the innkeeper's paunch and Matrena's white throat bathed in perspiration. "Kill I must, and it must be both!"

He heard the cock crow for the second time.

"I must do it at once, or dawn will be here." He had seen in the evening before he went to bed a knife and an axe. He crawled down from the stove, took the knife and axe, and went out of the kitchen door. At that very moment he heard the lock of the entrance door open. The innkeeper was going out of the house to the courtyard. It all turned out contrary to what Stepan desired. He had no opportunity of using the knife; he just swung the axe and split the innkeeper's head in two. The man tumbled down on the threshold of the door, then on the ground.

Stepan stepped into the bedroom. Matrena jumped out of bed, and remained standing by its side. With the same axe Stepan killed her also.

Then he lighted the candle, took the money out of the desk, and left the house.

XVI

In a small district town, some distance away from the other buildings, an old man, a former official, who had taken to drink, lived in his own house with his two daughters and his son-in-law. The married daughter was also addicted to drink and led a bad life, and it was the elder daughter, the widow Maria Semenovna, a wrinkled woman of fifty, who supported the whole family. She had a pension of two hundred and fifty roubles a year, and the family lived on this. Maria Semenovna did all the work in the house, looked after the drunken old father, who was very weak, attended to her sister's child, and managed all the cooking and the washing of the family. And, as is always the case, whatever there was to do, she was expected to do it, and was, moreover, continually scolded by all the three people in the house; her brother-in-law used even to beat her when he was drunk. She bore it all patiently, and as is also always the case, the more work she had to face, the quicker she managed to get through it. She helped the poor, sacrificing her own wants; she gave them her clothes, and was a ministering angel to the sick.

Once the lame, crippled village tailor was working in Maria Semenovna's house. He had to mend her old father's coat, and to mend and repair Maria Semenovna's fur-jacket for her to wear in winter when she went to market.

The lame tailor was a clever man, and a keen observer: he had seen many different people owing to his profession, and was fond of reflection, condemned as he was to a sedentary life.

Having worked a week at Maria Semenovna's, he wondered greatly about her life. One day she came to the kitchen, where he was sitting with his work, to wash a towel, and began to ask him how he was getting on. He told her of the wrong he had suffered from his brother, and how he now lived on his own allotment of land, separated from that of his brother.

"I thought I should have been better off that way," he said. "But I am now just as poor as before."

"It is much better never to change, but to take life as it comes," said Maria Semenovna. "Take life as it comes," she repeated.

"Why, I wonder at you, Maria Semenovna," said the lame tailor. "You alone do the work, and you are so good to everybody. But they don't repay you in kind, I see."

Maria Semenovna did not utter a word in answer.

"I dare say you have found out in books that we are rewarded in heaven for the good we do here."

"We don't know that. But we must try to do the best we can."

"Is it said so in books?"

"In books as well," she said, and read to him the Sermon on the Mount. The tailor was much impressed. When he had been paid for his job and gone home, he did not cease to think about Maria Semenovna, both what she had said and what she had read to him.

XVII

Peter Nikolaevich Sventizky's views of the peasantry had now changed for the worse, and the peasants had an equally bad opinion of him. In the course of a single year they felled twenty-seven oaks in his forest, and burnt a barn which had not been insured. Peter Nikolaevich came to the conclusion that there was no getting on with the people around him.

At that very time the landowner, Liventsov, was trying to find a manager for his estate, and the Marshal of the Nobility recommended Peter Nikolaevich as the ablest man in the district in the management of land. The estate owned by Liventsov was an extremely large one, but there was no revenue to be got out of it, as the peasants appropriated all its wealth to their own profit. Peter Nikolaevich undertook to bring everything into order; rented out his own land to somebody else; and settled with his wife on the Liventsov estate, in a distant province on the river Volga.

Peter Nikolaevich was always fond of order, and wanted things to be regulated by law; and now he felt less able of allowing those raw and rude peasants to take possession, quite illegally too, of property that did not belong to them. He was glad of the opportunity of giving them a good lesson, and set seriously to work at once. One peasant was sent to prison for stealing wood; to another he gave a thrashing for not having made way for him on the road with his cart, and for not having lifted his cap to salute him. As to the pasture ground which was a subject of dispute, and was considered by the peasants as their property, Peter Nikolaevich informed the peasants that any of their cattle grazing on it would be driven away by him.

The spring came and the peasants, just as they had done in previous years, drove their cattle on to the meadows belonging to the landowner. Peter Nikolaevich called some of the men working on the estate and ordered them to drive the cattle into his yard. The peasants were working in the fields, and, disregarding the screaming of the women, Peter

Nikolaevich's men succeeded in driving in the cattle. When they came home the peasants went in a crowd to the cattle-yard on the estate, and asked for their cattle. Peter Nikolaevich came out to talk to them with a gun slung on his shoulder; he had just returned from a ride of inspection. He told them that he would not let them have their cattle unless they paid a fine of fifty kopeks for each of the horned cattle, and twenty kopeks for each sheep. The peasants loudly declared that the pasture ground was their property, because their fathers and grandfathers had used it, and protested that he had no right whatever to lay hand on their cattle.

"Give back our cattle, or you will regret it," said an old man coming up to Peter Nikolaevich.

"How shall I regret it?" cried Peter Nikolaevich, turning pale, and coming close to the old man.

"Give them back, you villain, and don't provoke us."

"What?" cried Peter Nikolaevich, and slapped the old man in the face.

"You dare to strike me? Come along, you fellows, let us take back our cattle by force."

The crowd drew close to him. Peter Nikolaevich tried to push his way, through them, but the peasants resisted him. Again he tried force.

His gun, accidentally discharged in the melee, killed one of the peasants. Instantly the fight began. Peter Nikolaevich was trodden down, and five minutes later his mutilated body was dragged into the ravine.

The murderers were tried by martial law, and two of them sentenced to the gallows.

XVIII

In the village where the lame tailor lived, in the Zemliansk district of the Voronesh province, five rich peasants hired from the landowner a hundred and five acres of rich arable land, black as tar, and let it out on lease to the rest of the peasants at fifteen to eighteen roubles an acre. Not one acre was given under twelve roubles. They got a very profitable return, and the five acres which were left to each of their company practically cost them nothing. One of the five peasants died, and the lame tailor received an offer to take his place.

When they began to divide the land, the tailor gave up drinking vodka, and, being consulted as to how much land was to be divided, and to whom it should be given, he proposed to give allotments to all on equal terms, not taking from the tenants more than was due for each piece of land out of the sum paid to the landowner.

"Why so?"

"We are no heathens, I should think," he said. "It is all very well for the masters to be unfair, but we are true Christians. We must do as God bids. Such is the law of Christ."

"Where have you got that law from?"

"It is in the Book, in the Gospels; just come to me on Sunday, I will read you a few passages, and we will have a talk afterwards."

They did not all come to him on Sunday, but three came, and he began reading to them.

He read five chapters of St. Matthew's Gospel, and they talked. One man only, Ivan Chouev, accepted the lesson and carried it out completely, following the rule of Christ in everything from that day. His family did the same. Out of the arable land he took only what was his due, and refused to take more.

The lame tailor and Ivan had people calling on them, and some of these people began to grasp the meaning of the Gospels, and in consequence gave up smoking, drinking, swearing, and using bad language and tried to help one another. They also ceased to go to church, and took their ikons to the village priest, saying they did not want them any more. The priest was frightened, and reported what had occurred to the bishop. The bishop was at a loss what to do. At last he resolved to send the archimandrite Missael to the village, the one who had formerly been Mitia Smokovnikov's teacher of religion.

XIX

Asking Father Missael on his arrival to take a seat, the bishop told him what had happened in his diocese.

"It all comes from weakness of spirit and from ignorance. You are a learned man, and I rely on you. Go to the village, call the parishioners together, and convince them of their error."

"If your Grace bids me go, and you give me your blessing, I will do my best," said Father Missael. He was very pleased with the task entrusted to him. Every opportunity he could find to demonstrate the firmness of his faith was a boon to him. In trying to convince others he was chiefly intent on persuading himself that he was really a firm believer.

"Do your best. I am greatly distressed about my flock," said the bishop, leisurely taking a cup with his white plump hands from the servant who brought in the tea.

"Why is there only one kind of jam? Bring another," he said to the servant. "I am greatly distressed," he went on, turning to Father Missael.

Missael earnestly desired to prove his zeal; but, being a man of small means, he asked to be paid for the expenses of his journey; and being afraid of the rough people who might be ill-dis-posed towards him, he also asked the bishop to get him an order from the governor of the province, so that the local police might help him in case of need. The bishop complied with his wishes, and Missael got his things ready with the help of his servant and his cook. They furnished him with a case full of wine, and a basket with the victuals he might need in going to such a lonely place. Fully provided with all he wanted, he started for the village to which he was commissioned. He was pleasantly conscious of the importance of his mission. All his doubts as to his own faith passed away, and he was now fully convinced of its reality.

His thoughts, far from being concerned with the real foundation of his creed—this was accepted as an axiom—were occupied with the arguments used against the forms of worship.

XX

The village priest and his wife received Father Missael with great honours, and the next day after he had arrived the parishioners were invited to assemble in the church. Missael in a new silk cassock, with a large cross on his chest, and his long hair carefully combed, ascended the pulpit; the priest stood at his side, the deacons and the choir at a little distance behind him, and the side entrances were guarded by the police. The dissenters also came in their dirty sheepskin coats.

After the service Missael delivered a sermon, admonishing the dissenters to return to the bosom of their mother, the Church, threatening them with the torments of hell, and promising full forgiveness to those who would repent.

The dissenters kept silent at first. Then, being asked questions, they gave answers. To the question why they dissented, they said that their chief reason was the fact that the Church worshipped gods made of wood, which, far from being ordained, were condemned by the Scriptures.

When asked by Missael whether they actually considered the holy ikons to be mere planks of wood, Chouev answered,—"Just look at the back of any ikon you choose and you will see what they are made of."

When asked why they turned against the priests, their answer was that the Scripture says: "As you have received it without fee, so you must give it to the others; whereas the priests require payment for the grace they bestow by the sacraments." To all attempts which Missael made to oppose them by arguments founded on Holy Writ, the tailor and Ivan Chouev gave calm but very firm answers, contradicting his assertions by appeal to the Scriptures, which they knew uncommonly well.

Missael got angry and threatened them with persecution by the authorities. Their answer was: It is said, I have been persecuted and so will you be.

The discussion came to nothing, and all would have ended well if Missael had not preached the next day at mass, denouncing the wicked seducers of the faithful and saying that they deserved the worst punishment. Coming out of the church, the crowd of peasants began to consult whether it would not be well to give the infidels a good lesson for disturbing the minds of the community. The same day, just when Missael was enjoying some salmon and gangfish, dining at the village priest's in company with the inspector, a violent brawl arose in the village. The peasants came in a crowd to Chouev's cottage, and waited for the dissenters to come out in order to give them a thrashing.

The dissenters assembled in the cottage numbered about twenty men and women. Missael's sermon and the attitude of the orthodox peasants, together with their threats, aroused in the mind of the dissenters angry feelings, to which they had before been strangers. It was near evening, the women had to go and milk the cows, and the peasants were still standing and waiting at the door.

A boy who stepped out of the door was beaten and driven back into the house. The people within began consulting what was to be done, and could come to no agreement. The tailor said, "We must bear whatever is done to us, and not resist." Chouev replied that if they decided on that course they would, all of them, be beaten to death. In consequence, he seized a poker and went out of the house. "Come!" he shouted, "let us follow the law of Moses!" And, falling upon the peasants, he knocked out one man's eye, and in the meanwhile all those who had been in his house contrived to get out and make their way home.

Chouev was thrown into prison and charged with sedition and blasphemy.

XXI

Two years previous to those events a strong and handsome young girl of an eastern type, Katia Turchaninova, came from the Don military settlements to St. Petersburg to study in the university college for women. In that town she met a student, Turin, the son of a district governor in the Simbirsk province, and fell in love with him. But her love was not of the ordinary type, and she had no desire to become his wife and the mother of his children. He was a dear comrade to her, and their chief bond of union was a feeling of revolt they had in common, as well as the hatred they bore, not only to the existing forms of government, but to all those who represented that government. They had also in common the sense that they both excelled their enemies in culture, in brains, as well as in morals. Katia Turchaninova was a gifted girl, possessed of a good memory, by means of which she easily mastered the lectures she attended. She was successful in her examinations, and, apart from that, read all the newest books. She was certain that her vocation was not to bear and rear children, and even looked on such a task with disgust and contempt. She thought herself chosen by destiny to destroy the present government, which was fettering the best abilities of the nation, and to reveal to the people a higher standard of life, inculcated by the latest writers of other countries. She was handsome, a little inclined to stoutness: she had a good complexion, shining black eyes, abundant black hair. She inspired the men she knew with feelings she neither wished nor had time to share, busy as she was with propaganda work, which consisted chiefly in mere talking. She was not displeased, however, to inspire these feelings; and, without dressing too smartly, did not neglect her appearance. She liked to be admired, as it gave her opportunities of showing how little she prized what was valued so highly by other women.

In her views concerning the method of fighting the government she went further than the majority of her comrades, and than her friend Turin; all means, she taught, were justified in such a struggle, not excluding murder. And yet, with all her revolutionary ideas, Katia Turchaninova was in her soul a very kind girl, ready to sacrifice herself for the welfare and the happiness of other people, and sincerely pleased when she could do a kindness to anybody, a child, an old person, or an animal.

She went in the summer to stay with a friend, a schoolmistress in a small town on the river Volga. Turin lived near that town, on his father's estate. He often came to see the two girls; they gave each other books to read, and had long discussions, expressing their common indignation with the state of affairs in the country. The district doctor, a friend of theirs, used also to join them on many occasions.

The estate of the Turins was situated in the neighbourhood of the Liventsov estate, the one that was entrusted to the management of Peter Nikolaevich Sventizky. Soon after Peter Nikolaevich had settled there, and begun to enforce order, young Turin, having observed an independent tendency in the peasants on the Liventsov estate, as well as their determination to uphold their rights, became interested in them. He came often to the village to talk with the men, and developed his socialistic theories, insisting particularly on the nationalisation of the land.

After Peter Nikolaevich had been murdered, and the murderers sent to trial, the revolutionary group of the small town boiled over with indignation, and did not shrink from openly expressing it. The fact of Turin's visits to the village and his propaganda work among the students, became known to the authorities during the trial. A search was made in his house; and, as the police found a few revolutionary leaflets among his effects, he was arrested and transferred to prison in St. Petersburg.

Katia Turchaninova followed him to the metropolis, and went to visit him in prison. She was not admitted on the day she came, and was told to come on the day fixed by regulations for visits to the prisoners. When that day arrived, and she was finally allowed to see him, she had to talk to him through two gratings separating the prisoner from his visitor. This visit increased her indignation against the authorities. And her feelings become all the more revolutionary after a visit she paid to the office of a gendarme officer who had to deal with the Turin case. The officer, a handsome man, seemed obviously disposed to grant her exceptional favours in visiting the prisoner, if she would allow him to make love to her. Disgusted with him, she appealed to the chief of police. He pretended—just as the officer did when talking officially to her—to be powerless himself, and to depend entirely on orders coming from the minister of state. She sent a petition to the minister asking for an interview, which was refused.

Then she resolved to do a desperate thing and bought a revolver.

XXII

The minister was receiving petitioners at the usual hour appointed for the reception. He had talked successively to three of them, and now a pretty young woman with black eyes, who was holding a petition in her left hand, approached. The minister's eyes gleamed when he saw how attractive the petitioner was, but recollecting his high position he put on a serious face.

"What do you want?" he asked, coming down to where she stood. Without answering his question the young woman quickly drew a revolver from under her cloak and aiming it at the minister's chest fired—but missed him.

The minister rushed at her, trying to seize her hand, but she escaped, and taking a step back, fired a second time. The minister ran out of the room. The woman was immediately seized. She was trembling violently, and could not utter a single word; after a while she suddenly burst into a hysterical laugh. The minister was not even wounded.

That woman was Katia Turchaninova. She was put into the prison of preliminary detention. The minister received congratulations and marks of sympathy from the highest quarters, and even from the emperor himself, who appointed a commission to investigate the plot that had led to the attempted assassination. As a matter of fact there was no plot whatever, but the police officials and the detectives set to work with the utmost zeal to discover all the threads of the non-existing conspiracy. They did everything to deserve the fees they were paid; they got up in the small hours of the morning, searched one house after another, took copies of papers and of books they found, read diaries, personal letters, made extracts from them on the very best notepaper and in beautiful handwriting, interrogated Katia Turchaninova ever so many times, and confronted her with all those whom they suspected of conspiracy, in order to extort from her the names of her accomplices.

The minister, a good-natured man at heart, was sincerely sorry for the pretty girl. But he said to himself that he was bound to consider his high state duties imposed upon him, even though they did not imply much work and trouble. So, when his former colleague, a chamberlain and a friend of the Turins, met him at a court ball and tried to rouse his pity for Turin and the girl Turchaninova, he shrugged his shoulders, stretching the red ribbon on his white waistcoat, and said: "Je ne demanderais pas mieux que de relacher cette pauvre fillette, mais vous savez le devoir." And in the meantime Katia Turchaninova was kept in prison. She was at times in a quiet mood, communicated with her fellow-prisoners by knocking on the walls, and read the books that were sent to her. But then came days when she had fits of desperate fury, knocking with her fists against the wall, screaming and laughing like a mad-woman.

XXIII

One day Maria Semenovna came home from the treasurer's office, where she had received her pension. On her way she met a schoolmaster, a friend of hers.

"Good day, Maria Semenovna! Have you received your money?" the schoolmaster asked, in a loud voice from the other side of the street.

"I have," answered Maria Semenovna. "But it was not much; just enough to fill the holes."

"Oh, there must be some tidy pickings out of such a lot of money," said the schoolmaster, and passed on, after having said good-bye.

"Good-bye," said Maria Semenovna. While she was looking at her friend, she met a tall man face to face, who had very long arms and a stern look in his eyes. Coming to her house, she was very startled on again seeing the same man with the long arms, who had evidently followed her. He remained standing another moment after she had gone in, then turned and walked away.

Maria Semenovna felt somewhat frightened at first. But when she had entered the house, and had given her father and her nephew Fedia the presents she had brought for them, and she had patted the dog Treasure, who whined with joy, she forgot her fears. She gave the money to her father and began to work, as there was always plenty for her to do.

The man she met face to face was Stepan.

After he had killed the innkeeper, he did not return to town. Strange to say, he was not sorry to have committed that murder. His mind went back to the murdered man over and over again during the following day; and he liked the recollection of having done the thing so skilfully, so cleverly, that nobody would ever discover it, and he would not therefore be prevented from murdering other people in the same way. Sitting in the public-house and having his tea, he looked at the people around him with the same thought how he should murder them. In the evening he called at a carter's, a man from his village, to spend the night at his house. The carter was not in. He said he would wait for him, and in the meanwhile began talking to the carter's wife. But when she moved to the stove, with her back turned to him, the idea entered his mind to kill her. He marvelled at himself at first, and shook his head; but the next moment he seized the knife he had hidden in his boot, knocked the woman down on the floor, and cut her throat. When the children began to scream, he killed them also and went away. He did not look out for another place to spend the night, but at once left the town. In a village some distance away he went to the inn and slept there. The next day he returned to the district town, and there he overheard in the street Maria Semenovna's talk with the schoolmaster. Her look frightened him, but yet he made up his mind to creep into her house, and rob her of the money she had received. When the night came he broke the lock and entered the house. The first person who heard his steps was the younger daughter, the married one. She screamed. Stepan stabbed her immediately with his knife. Her husband woke up and fell upon Stepan, seized him by his throat, and struggled with him desperately. But Stepan was the stronger man and overpowered him. After murdering him, Stepan, excited by the long fight, stepped into the next room behind a partition. That was Maria Semenovna's bedroom. She rose in her bed, looked at Stepan with her mild frightened eyes, and crossed herself.

Once more her look scared Stepan. He dropped his eyes.

"Where is your money?" he asked, without raising his face.

She did not answer.

"Where is the money?" asked Stepan again, showing her his knife.

"How can you . . ." she said.

"You will see how."

Stepan came close to her, in order to seize her hands and prevent her struggling with him, but she did not even try to lift her arms or offer any resistance; she pressed her hands to her chest, and sighed heavily.

"Oh, what a great sin!" she cried. "How can you! Have mercy on yourself. To destroy somebody's soul . . . and worse, your own! . . ."

Stepan could not stand her voice any longer, and drew his knife sharply across her throat. "Stop that talk!" he said. She fell back with a hoarse cry, and the pillow was stained with blood. He turned away, and went round the rooms in order to collect all he thought worth taking. Having made a bundle of the most valuable things, he lighted a cigarette, sat down for a while, brushed his clothes, and left the house. He thought this murder would not matter to him more than those he had committed before; but before he got a night's lodging, he felt suddenly so exhausted that he could not walk any farther. He stepped down into the gutter and remained lying there the rest of the night, and the next day and the next night.

SECOND PART

I

The whole time he was lying in the gutter Stepan saw continually before his eyes the thin, kindly, and frightened face of Maria Semenovna, and seemed to hear her voice. "How can you?" she went on saying in his imagination, with her peculiar lisping voice. Stepan saw over again and over again before him all he had done to her. In horror he shut his eyes, and shook his hairy head, to drive away these thoughts and recollections. For a moment he would get rid of them, but in their place horrid black faces with red eyes appeared and frightened him continuously. They grinned at him, and kept repeating, "Now you have done away with her you must do away with yourself, or we will not leave you alone." He opened his eyes, and again he saw *her* and heard her voice; and felt an immense pity for her and a deep horror and disgust with himself. Once more he shut his eyes, and the black faces reappeared. Towards the evening of the next day he rose and went, with hardly any strength left, to a public-house. There he ordered a drink, and repeated his demands over and over again, but no quantity of liquor could make him intoxicated. He was sitting at a table, and swallowed silently one glass after another.

A police officer came in. "Who are you?" he asked Stepan.

"I am the man who murdered all the Dobrotvorov people last night," he answered.

He was arrested, bound with ropes, and brought to the nearest police-station; the next day he was transferred to the prison in the town. The inspector of the prison recognised him as an old inmate, and a very turbulent one; and, hearing that he had now become a real criminal, accosted him very harshly.

"You had better be quiet here," he said in a hoarse voice, frowning, and protruding his lower jaw. "The moment you don't behave, I'll flog you to death! Don't try to escape—I will see to that!"

"I have no desire to escape," said Stepan, dropping his eyes. "I surrendered of my own free will."

71

"Shut up! You must look straight into your superior's eyes when you talk to him," cried the inspector, and struck Stepan with his fist under the jaw.

At that moment Stepan again saw the murdered woman before him, and heard her voice; he did not pay attention, therefore, to the inspector's words.

"What?" he asked, coming to his senses when he felt the blow on his face.

"Be off! Don't pretend you don't hear."

The inspector expected Stepan to be violent, to talk to the other prisoners, to make attempts to escape from prison. But nothing of the kind ever happened. Whenever the guard or the inspector himself looked into his cell through the hole in the door, they saw Stepan sitting on a bag filled with straw, holding his head with his hands and whispering to himself. On being brought before the examining magistrate charged with the inquiry into his case, he did not behave like an ordinary convict. He was very absent-minded, hardly listening to the questions; but when he heard what was asked, he answered truthfully, causing the utmost perplexity to the magistrate, who, accustomed as he was to the necessity of being very clever and very cunning with convicts, felt a strange sensation just as if he were lifting up his foot to ascend a step and found none. Stepan told him the story of all his murders; and did it frowning, with a set look, in a quiet, businesslike voice, trying to recollect all the circumstances of his crimes. "He stepped out of the house," said Stepan, telling the tale of his first murder, "and stood barefooted at the door; I hit him, and he just groaned; I went to his wife, . . ." And so on.

One day the magistrate, visiting the prison cells, asked Stepan whether there was anything he had to complain of, or whether he had any wishes that might be granted him. Stepan said he had no wishes whatever, and had nothing to complain of the way he was treated in prison. The magistrate, on leaving him, took a few steps in the foul passage, then stopped and asked the governor who had accompanied him in his visit how this prisoner was behaving.

"I simply wonder at him," said the governor, who was very pleased with Stepan, and spoke kindly of him. "He has now been with us about two months, and could be held up as a model of good behaviour. But I am afraid he is plotting some mischief. He is a daring man, and exceptionally strong."

II

During the first month in prison Stepan suffered from the same agonising vision. He saw the grey wall of his cell, he heard the sounds of the prison; the noise of the cell below him, where a number of convicts were confined together; the striking of the prison clock; the steps of the sentry in the passage; but at the same time he saw _her_ with that kindly face which conquered his heart the very first time he met her in the street, with that thin, strongly-marked neck, and he heard her soft, lisping, pathetic voice: "To destroy somebody's soul . . . and, worst of all, your own. . . . How can you? . . ."

After a while her voice would die away, and then black faces would appear. They would appear whether he had his eyes open or shut. With his closed eyes he saw them more distinctly. When he opened his eyes they vanished for a moment, melting away into the walls and the door; but after a while they reappeared and surrounded him from three sides, grinning at him and saying over and over: "Make an end! Make an end! Hang yourself! Set yourself on fire!" Stepan shook all over when he heard that, and tried to say all the prayers he knew: "Our Lady" or "Our Father." At first this seemed to help. In saying his prayers he began to recollect his whole life; his father, his mother, the village, the dog "Wolf," the old grandfather lying on the stove, the bench on which the children used to play; then the girls in the village with their songs, his horses and how they had been stolen, and how the thief was caught and how he killed him with a stone. He recollected also the first prison he was in and his leaving it, and the fat innkeeper, the carter's wife and the children. Then again _she_ came to his mind and again he was terrified. Throwing his prison overcoat off his shoulders, he jumped out of bed, and, like a wild animal in a cage, began pacing up and down his tiny cell, hastily turning round when he had reached the damp walls. Once more he tried to pray, but it was of no use now.

The autumn came with its long nights. One evening when the wind whistled and howled in the pipes, Stepan, after he had paced up and down his cell for a long time, sat down on his bed. He felt he could not struggle any more; the black demons had overpowered him, and he had to submit. For some time he had been looking at the funnel of the oven. If he could fix on the knob of its lid a loop made of thin shreds of narrow linen straps it would hold. . . . But he would have to manage it very cleverly. He set to work, and spent two days in making straps out of the linen bag on which he slept. When the guard came into the cell he covered the bed with his overcoat. He tied the straps with big knots and made them double, in order that they might be strong enough to hold his weight. During these preparations he was free from tormenting visions. When the straps were ready he made a slip-knot out of them, and put it round his neck, stood up in his bed, and hanged himself. But at the very moment that his tongue began to protrude the straps got loose, and he fell down. The guard rushed in at the noise. The doctor was called in, Stepan was brought to the infirmary. The next day he recovered, and was removed from the infirmary, no more to solitary confinement, but to share the common cell with other prisoners.

In the common cell he lived in the company of twenty men, but felt as if he were quite alone. He did not notice the presence of the rest; did not speak to anybody, and was tormented by the old agony. He felt it most of all when the men were sleeping and he alone could not get one moment of sleep. Continually he saw *her* before his eyes, heard her voice, and then again the black devils with their horrible eyes came and tortured him in the usual way.

He again tried to say his prayers, but, just as before, it did not help him. One day when, after his prayers, she was again before his eyes, he began to implore her dear soul to forgive him his sin, and release him. Towards morning, when he fell down quite exhausted on his crushed linen bag, he fell asleep at once, and in his dream she came to him with her thin, wrinkled, and severed neck. "Will you forgive me?" he asked. She looked at him with her mild eyes and did not answer. "Will you forgive me?" And so he asked her three times. But she did not say a word, and he awoke. From that time onwards he suffered less, and seemed to come to his senses, looked around him, and began for the first time to talk to the other men in the cell.

III

Stepan's cell was shared among others by the former yard-porter, Vassily, who had been sentenced to deportation for robbery, and by Chouev, sentenced also to deportation. Vassily sang songs the whole day long with his fine voice, or told his adventures to the other men in the cell. Chouev was working at something all day, mending his clothes, or reading the Gospel and the Psalter.

Stepan asked him why he was put into prison, and Chouev answered that he was being persecuted because of his true Christian faith by the priests, who were all of them hypocrites and hated those who followed the law of Christ. Stepan asked what that true law was, and Chouev made clear to him that the true law consists in not worshipping gods made with hands, but worshipping the spirit and the truth. He told him how he had learnt the truth from the lame tailor at the time when they were dividing the land.

"And what will become of those who have done evil?" asked Stepan.

"The Scriptures give an answer to that," said Chouev, and read aloud to him Matthew xxv. 31:—"When the Son of Man shall come in His glory, and all the holy angels with Him, then shall He sit upon the throne of His glory: and before Him shall be gathered all nations: and He shall separate them one from another, as a shepherd divideth His sheep from the goats: and He shall set the sheep on His right hand, but the goats on the left. Then shall the King say unto them on His right hand, Come, ye blessed of My Father, inherit the kingdom prepared for you from the foundation of the world: for I was an hungred, and ye gave Me meat: I was thirsty, and ye gave Me drink: I was a stranger, and ye took Me in: naked, and ye clothed Me: I was sick, and ye visited Me: I was in prison, and ye came unto Me. Then shall the righteous answer Him, saying, Lord, when saw we Thee an hungred, and fed Thee? or thirsty, and gave Thee drink? When saw we Thee a stranger, and took Thee in? or naked, and clothed Thee? Or when saw we Thee sick, or in prison, and came unto Thee? And the King shall answer and say unto them, Verily I say unto you, inasmuch as ye have done it unto one of the least of these My brethren, ye have done it unto Me. Then shall He say also unto them on the left hand, Depart from Me, ye cursed, into everlasting fire, prepared for the devil and his angels: for I was an hungred, and ye gave Me no meat: I was thirsty, and ye gave Me no drink: I was a stranger and ye took Me not in: naked, and ye clothed Me not; sick, and in prison, and ye visited Me not. Then shall they also answer Him, saying, Lord, when saw we Thee an hungred, or athirst, or a stranger, or naked, or sick, or in prison, and did not minister unto Thee? Then shall He answer them, saying, Verily I say unto you, Inasmuch as ye did it not to one of the least of these, ye did it not to Me. And these shall go away into everlasting punishment: but the righteous into life eternal."

Vassily, who was sitting on the floor at Chouev's side, and was listening to his reading the Gospel, nodded his handsome head in approval. "True," he said in a resolute tone. "Go, you cursed villains, into everlasting punishment, since you did not give food to the hungry, but swallowed it all yourself. Serves them right! I have read the holy Nikodim's writings," he added, showing off his erudition.

"And will they never be pardoned?" asked Stepan, who had listened silently, with his hairy head bent low down.

"Wait a moment, and be silent," said Chouev to Vassily, who went on talking about the rich who had not given meat to the stranger, nor visited him in the prison.

"Wait, I say!" said Chouev, again turning over the leaves of the Gospel. Having found what he was looking for, Chouev smoothed the page with his large and strong hand, which had become exceedingly white in prison:

"And there were also two other malefactors, led with Him"—it means with Christ—"to be put to death. And when they were come to the place, which is called Calvary, there they crucified Him, and the malefactors, one on the right hand, and the other on the left. Then said Jesus,—'Father, forgive them; for they know not what they do.' And the people stood beholding. And the rulers also with them derided Him, saying,—'He saved others; let Him save Himself if He be Christ, the chosen of God.' And the soldiers also mocked Him, coming to Him, and offering Him vinegar, and saying, 'If Thou be the King of the Jews save Thyself.' And a superscription also was written over Him in letters of Greek, and Latin, and Hebrew, 'This is the King of the Jews.' And one of the malefactors which were hanged railed on Him, saying, 'If thou be Christ, save Thyself and us.' But the other answering rebuked Him, saying, 'Dost not thou fear God, seeing thou art in the same condemnation? And we indeed justly, for we receive the due reward of our deeds: but this man hath done nothing amiss.' And he said unto Jesus, 'Lord, remember me when Thou comest into Thy kingdom.' And Jesus said unto him, 'Verily I say unto thee, to-day shalt thou be with Me in paradise.'"

Stepan did not say anything, and was sitting in thought, as if he were listening.

Now he knew what the true faith was. Those only will be saved who have given food and drink to the poor and visited the prisoners; those who have not done it, go to hell. And yet the malefactor had repented on the cross, and went nevertheless to paradise. This did not strike him as being inconsistent. Quite the contrary. The one confirmed the other: the fact that the merciful will go to Heaven, and the unmerciful to hell, meant that everybody ought to be merciful, and the malefactor having been forgiven by Christ meant that Christ was merciful. This was all new to Stepan, and he wondered why it had been hidden from him so long.

From that day onward he spent all his free time with Chouev, asking him questions and listening to him. He saw but a single truth at the bottom of the teaching of Christ as revealed to him by Chouev: that all men are brethren, and that they ought to love and pity one another in order that all might be happy. And when he listened to Chouev, everything that was consistent with this fundamental truth came to him like a thing he had known before and only forgotten since, while whatever he heard that seemed to contradict it, he would take no notice of, as he thought that he simply had not understood the real meaning. And from that time Stepan was a different man.

IV

Stepan had been very submissive and meek ever since he came to the prison, but now he made the prison authorities and all his fellow-prisoners wonder at the change in him. Without being ordered, and out of his proper turn he would do all the very hardest work in prison, and the dirtiest too. But in spite of his humility, the other prisoners stood in awe of him, and were afraid of him, as they knew he was a resolute man, possessed of great physical strength. Their respect for him increased after the incident of the two tramps who fell upon him; he wrenched himself loose from them and broke the arm of one of them in the fight. These tramps had gambled with a young prisoner of some means and deprived him of all his money. Stepan took his part, and deprived the tramps of their winnings. The tramps poured their abuse on him; but when they attacked him, he got the better of them. When the Governor asked how the fight had come about, the tramps declared that it was Stepan who had begun it. Stepan did not try to exculpate himself, and bore patiently his sentence which was three days in the punishment-cell, and after that solitary confinement.

In his solitary cell he suffered because he could no longer listen to Chouev and his Gospel. He was also afraid that the former visions of her and of the black devils would reappear to torment him. But the visions were gone for good. His soul was full of new and happy ideas. He felt glad to be alone if only he could read, and if he had the Gospel. He knew that he might have got hold of the Gospel, but he could not read.

He had started to learn the alphabet in his boyhood, but could not grasp the joining of the syllables, and remained illiterate. He made up his mind to start reading anew, and asked the guard to bring him the Gospels. They were brought to him, and he sat down to work. He contrived to recollect the letters, but could not join them into syllables. He tried as hard as he could to understand how the letters ought to be put together to form words, but with no result whatever. He lost his sleep, had no desire to eat, and a deep sadness came over him, which he was unable to shake off.

"Well, have you not yet mastered it?" asked the guard one day.

"No."

"Do you know 'Our Father'?"

"I do."

"Since you do, read it in the Gospels. Here it is," said the guard, showing him the prayer in the Gospels. Stepan began to read it, comparing the letters he knew with the familiar sounds.

And all of a sudden the mystery of the syllables was revealed to him, and he began to read. This was a great joy. From that moment he could read, and the meaning of the words, spelt out with such great pains, became more significant.

Stepan did not mind any more being alone. He was so full of his work that he did not feel glad when he was transferred back to the common cell, his private cell being needed for a political prisoner who had been just sent to prison.

V

In the meantime Mahin, the schoolboy who had taught his friend Smokovnikov to forge the coupon, had finished his career at school and then at the university, where he had studied law. He had the advantage of being liked by women, and as he had won favour with a vice-minister's former mistress, he was appointed when still young as examining magistrate. He was dishonest, had debts, had gambled, and had seduced many women; but he was clever, sagacious, and a good magistrate. He was appointed to the court of the district where Stepan Pelageushkine had been tried. When Stepan was brought to him the first time to give evidence, his sincere and quiet answers puzzled the magistrate. He somehow unconsciously felt that this man, brought to him in fetters and with a shorn head, guarded by two soldiers who were waiting to take him back to prison, had a free soul and was immeasurably superior to himself. He was in consequence somewhat troubled, and had to summon up all his courage in order to go on with the inquiry and not blunder in his questions. He was amazed that Stepan should narrate the story of his crimes as if they had been things of long ago, and committed not by him but by some different man.

"Had you no pity for them?" asked Mahin.

"No. I did not know then."

"Well, and now?"

Stepan smiled with a sad smile. "Now," he said, "I would not do it even if I were to be burned alive."

"But why?

"Because I have come to know that all men are brethren."

"What about me? Am I your brother also?"

"Of course you are."

"And how is it that I, your brother, am sending you to hard labour?"

"It is because you don't know."

"What do I not know?"

"Since you judge, it means obviously that you don't know."

"Go on. . . . What next?"

VI

Now it was not Chouev, but Stepan who used to read the gospel in the common cell. Some of the prisoners were singing coarse songs, while others listened to Stepan reading the gospel and talking about what he had read. The most attentive among those who listened were two of the prisoners, Vassily, and a convict called Mahorkin, a murderer who had become a hangman. Twice during his stay in this prison he was called upon to do duty as hangman, and both times in far-away places where nobody could be found to execute the sentences.

Two of the peasants who had killed Peter Nikolaevich Sventizky, had been sentenced to the gallows, and Mahorkin was ordered to go to Pensa to hang them. On all previous occasions he used to write a petition to the governor of the province—he knew well how to read and to write—stating that he had been ordered to fulfil his duty, and asking for money for his expenses. But now, to the greatest astonishment of the prison authorities, he said he did not intend to go, and added that he would not be a hangman any more.

"And what about being flogged?" cried the governor of the prison.

"I will have to bear it, as the law commands us not to kill."

"Did you get that from Pelageushkine? A nice sort of a prison prophet! You just wait and see what this will cost you!"

When Mahin was told of that incident, he was greatly impressed by the fact of Stepan's influence on the hangman, who refused to do his duty, running the risk of being hanged himself for insubordination.

VII

At an evening party at the Eropkins, Mahin, who was paying attentions to the two young daughters of the house—they were rich matches, both of them—having earned great applause for his fine singing and playing the piano, began telling the company about the strange convict who had converted the hangman. Mahin told his story very accurately, as he had a very good memory, which was all the more retentive because of his total indifference to those with whom he had to deal. He never paid the slightest attention to other people's feelings, and was therefore better able to keep all they did or said in his memory. He got interested in Stepan Pelageushkine, and, although he did not thoroughly understand him, yet asked himself involuntarily what was the matter with the man? He could not find an answer, but feeling that there was certainly something remarkable going on in Stepan's soul, he told the company at the Eropkins all about Stepan's conversion of the hangman, and also about his strange behaviour in prison, his reading the Gospels and his great influence on the rest of the prisoners. All this made a special impression on the younger daughter of the family, Lisa, a girl of eighteen, who was just recovering from the artificial life she had been living in a boarding-school; she felt as if she had emerged out of water, and was taking in the fresh air of true life with ecstasy. She asked Mahin to tell her more about the man Pelageushkine, and to explain to her how such a great change had come over him. Mahin told her what he knew from the police official about Stepan's last murder, and also what he had heard from Pelageushkine himself—how he had been conquered by the humility, mildness, and fearlessness of a kind woman, who had been his last victim, and how his eyes had been opened, while the reading of the Gospels had completed the change in him.

Lisa Eropkin was not able to sleep that night. For a couple of months a struggle had gone on in her heart between society life, into which her sister was dragging her, and her infatuation for Mahin, combined with a desire to reform him. This second desire now became the stronger. She had already heard about poor Maria Semenovna. But, after that kind woman had been murdered in such a ghastly way, and after Mahin, who learnt it from Stepan, had communicated to her all the facts concerning Maria Semenovna's life, Lisa herself passionately desired to become like her. She was a rich girl, and was afraid that Mahin had been courting her because of her money. So she resolved to give all she possessed to the poor, and told Mahin about it.

Mahin was very glad to prove his disinterestedness, and told Lisa that he loved her and not her money. Such proof of his innate nobility made him admire himself greatly. Mahin helped Lisa to carry out her decision. And the more he did so, the more he came to realise the new world of Lisa's spiritual ambitions, quite unknown to him heretofore.

VIII

All were silent in the common cell. Stepan was lying in his bed, but was not yet asleep. Vassily approached him, and, pulling him by his leg, asked him in a whisper to get up and to come to him. Stepan stepped out of his bed, and came up to Vassily.

"Do me a kindness, brother," said Vassily. "Help me!"

"In what?"

"I am going to fly from the prison."

Vassily told Stepan that he had everything ready for his flight.

"To-morrow I shall stir them up—" He pointed to the prisoners asleep in their beds. "They will give me away, and I shall be transferred to the cell in the upper floor. I know my way from there. What I want you for is to unscrew the prop in the door of the mortuary." "I can do that. But where will you go?"

"I don't care where. Are not there plenty of wicked people in every place?"

"Quite so, brother. But it is not our business to judge them."

"I am not a murderer, to be sure. I have not destroyed a living soul in my life. As for stealing, I don't see any harm in that. As if they have not robbed us!"

"Let them answer for it themselves, if they do."

"Bother them all! Suppose I rob a church, who will be hurt? This time I will take care not to break into a small shop, but will get hold of a lot of money, and then I will help people with it. I will give it to all good people."

One of the prisoners rose in his bed and listened. Stepan and Vassily broke off their conversation. The next day Vassily carried out his idea. He began complaining of the bread in prison, saying it was moist, and induced the prisoners to call the governor and to tell him of their discontent. The governor came, abused them all, and when he heard it was Vassily who had stirred up the men, he ordered him to be transferred into solitary confinement in the cell on the upper floor. This was all Vassily wanted.

IX

Vassily knew well that cell on the upper floor. He knew its floor, and began at once to take out bits of it. When he had managed to get under the floor he took out pieces of the ceiling beneath, and jumped down into the mortuary a floor below. That day only one corpse was lying on the table. There in the corner of the room were stored bags to make hay mattresses for the prisoners. Vassily knew about the bags, and that was why the mortuary served his purposes. The prop in the door had been unscrewed and put in again. He took it out, opened the door, and went out into the passage to the lavatory which was being built. In the lavatory was a large hole connecting the third floor with the basement floor. After having found the door of the lavatory he went back to the mortuary, stripped the sheet off the dead body which was as cold as ice (in taking off the sheet Vassily touched his hand), took the bags, tied them together to make a rope, and carried the rope to the lavatory. Then he attached it to the cross-beam, and climbed down along it. The rope did not reach the ground, but he did not know how much was wanting. Anyhow, he had to take the risk. He remained hanging in the air, and then jumped down. His legs were badly hurt, but he could still walk on. The basement had two windows; he could have climbed out of one of them but for the grating protecting them. He had to break the grating, but there was no tool to do it with. Vassily began to look around him, and chanced on a piece of plank with a sharp edge; armed with that weapon he tried to loosen the bricks which held the grating. He worked a long time at that task. The cock crowed for the second time, but the grating still held. At last he had loosened one side; and then he pushed the plank under the loosened end and pressed with all his force. The grating gave way completely, but at that moment one of the bricks fell down heavily. The noise could have been heard by the sentry. Vassily stood motionless. But silence reigned. He climbed out of the window. His way of escape was to climb the wall. An outhouse stood in the corner of the courtyard. He had to reach its roof, and pass thence to the top of the wall. But he would not be able to reach the roof without the help of the plank; so he had to go back through the basement window to fetch it. A moment later he came out of the window with the plank in his hands; he stood still for a while listening to the steps of the sentry. His expectations were justified. The sentry was walking up and down on the other side of the courtyard. Vassily came up to the outhouse, leaned the plank against it, and began climbing. The plank slipped and fell on the ground. Vassily had his stockings on; he took them off so that he could cling with his bare feet in coming down. Then he leaned the plank again against the house, and seized the water-pipe with his hands. If only this time the plank would hold! A quick movement up the water-pipe, and his knee rested on the roof. The sentry was approaching. Vassily lay motionless. The sentry did not notice him, and passed on. Vassily leaped to his feet; the iron roof cracked under him. Another step or two, and he would reach the wall. He could touch it with his hand now. He leaned forward with one hand, then with the other, stretched out his body as far as he could, and found himself on the wall. Only, not to break his legs in jumping down, Vassily turned round, remained hanging in the air by his hands, stretched himself out, loosened the grip of one hand, then the other. "Help, me, God!" He was on the ground. And the ground was soft. His legs were not hurt, and he ran at the top of his speed. In a suburb, Malania opened her door, and he crept under her warm coverlet, made of small pieces of different colours stitched together.

X

The wife of Peter Nikolaevich Sventizky, a tall and handsome woman, as quiet and sleek as a well-fed heifer, had seen from her window how her husband had been murdered and dragged away into the fields. The horror of such a sight to Natalia Ivanovna was so intense—how could it be otherwise?—that all her other feelings vanished. No sooner had the crowd disappeared from view behind the garden fence, and the voices had become still; no sooner had the barefooted Malania, their servant, run in with her eyes starting out of her head, calling out in a voice more suited to the proclamation of glad tidings the news that Peter Nikolaevich had been murdered and thrown into the ravine, than Natalia Ivanovna felt that behind her first sensation of horror, there was another sensation; a feeling of joy at her deliverance from the tyrant, who through all the nineteen years of their married life had made her work without a moment's rest. Her joy made her aghast; she did not confess it to herself, but hid it the more from those around. When his mutilated, yellow and hairy body was being washed and put into the coffin, she cried with horror, and wept and sobbed. When the coroner—a special coroner for serious cases—came and was taking her evidence, she noticed in the room, where the inquest was taking place, two peasants in irons, who had been charged as the principal culprits. One of them was an old man with a curly white beard, and a calm and severe countenance. The other was rather young, of a gipsy type, with bright eyes and curly dishevelled hair. She declared that they were the two men who had first seized hold of Peter Nikolaevich's hands. In spite of the gipsy-like peasant looking at her with his eyes glistening from under his moving eyebrows, and saying reproachfully: "A great sin, lady, it is. Remember your death hour!"—in spite of that, she did not feel at all sorry for them. On the contrary, she began to hate them during the inquest, and wished desperately to take revenge on her husband's murderers.

A month later, after the case, which was committed for trial by court-martial, had ended in eight men being sentenced to hard labour, and in two—the old man with the white beard, and the gipsy boy, as she called the other—being condemned to be hanged, Natalia felt vaguely uneasy. But unpleasant doubts soon pass away under the solemnity of a trial. Since such high authorities considered that this was the right thing to do, it must be right.

The execution was to take place in the village itself. One Sunday Malania came home from church in her new dress and her new boots, and announced to her mistress that the gallows were being erected, and that the hangman was expected from Moscow on Wednesday. She also announced that the families of the convicts were raging, and that their cries could be heard all over the village.

Natalia Ivanovna did not go out of her house; she did not wish to see the gallows and the people in the village; she only wanted what had to happen to be over quickly. She only considered her own feelings, and did not care for the convicts and their families.

On Tuesday the village constable called on Natalia Ivanovna. He was a friend, and she offered him vodka and preserved mushrooms of her own making. The constable, after eating a little, told her that the execution was not to take place the next day.

"Why?"

"A very strange thing has happened. There is no hangman to be found. They had one in Moscow, my son told me, but he has been reading the Gospels a good deal and says: 'I will not commit a murder.' He had himself been sentenced to hard labour for having committed a murder, and now he objects to hang when the law orders him. He was threatened with flogging. 'You may flog me,' he said, 'but I won't do it.'"

Natalia Ivanovna grew red and hot at the thought which suddenly came into her head.

"Could not the death sentence be commuted now?"

"How so, since the judges have passed it? The Czar alone has the right of amnesty."

"But how would he know?"

"They have the right of appealing to him."

"But it is on my account they are to die," said that stupid woman, Natalia Ivanovna. "And I forgive them."

The constable laughed. "Well—send a petition to the Czar."

"May I do it?"

"Of course you may."

"But is it not too late?"

"Send it by telegram."

"To the Czar himself?"

"To the Czar, if you like."

The story of the hangman having refused to do his duty, and preferring to take the flogging instead, suddenly changed the soul of Natalia Ivanovna. The pity and the horror she felt the moment she heard that the peasants were sentenced to death, could not be stifled now, but filled her whole soul.

"Filip Vassilievich, my friend. Write that telegram for me. I want to appeal to the Czar to pardon them."

The constable shook his head. "I wonder whether that would not involve us in trouble?"

"I do it upon my own responsibility. I will not mention your name."

"Is not she a kind woman," thought the constable. "Very kind-hearted, to be sure. If my wife had such a heart, our life would be a paradise, instead of what it is now." And he wrote the telegram,— "To his Imperial Majesty, the Emperor. Your Majesty's loyal subject, the widow of Peter Nikolaevich Sventizky, murdered by the peasants, throws herself at the sacred feet (this sentence, when he wrote it down, pleased the constable himself most of all) of your Imperial Majesty, and implores you to grant an amnesty to the peasants so and so, from such a province, district, and village, who have been sentenced to death."

The telegram was sent by the constable himself, and Natalia Ivanovna felt relieved and happy. She had a feeling that since she, the widow of the murdered man, had forgiven the murderers, and was applying for an amnesty, the Czar could not possibly refuse it.

XI

Lisa Eropkin lived in a state of continual excitement. The longer she lived a true Christian life as it had been revealed to her, the more convinced she became that it was the right way, and her heart was full of joy.

She had two immediate aims before her. The one was to convert Mahin; or, as she put it to herself, to arouse his true nature, which was good and kind. She loved him, and the light of her love revealed the divine element in his soul which is at the bottom of all souls. But, further, she saw in him an exceptionally kind and tender heart, as well as a noble mind. Her other aim was to abandon her riches. She had first thought of giving away what she possessed in order to test Mahin; but afterwards she wanted to do so for her own sake, for the sake of her own soul. She began by simply giving money to any one who wanted it. But her father stopped that; besides which, she felt disgusted at the crowd of supplicants who personally, and by letters, besieged her with demands for money. Then she resolved to apply to an old man, known to be a saint by his life, and to give him her money to dispose of in the way he thought best. Her father got angry with her when he heard about it. During a violent altercation he called her mad, a raving lunatic, and said he would take measures to prevent her from doing injury to herself.

Her father's irritation proved contagious. Losing all control over herself, and sobbing with rage, she behaved with the greatest impertinence to her father, calling him a tyrant and a miser.

Then she asked his forgiveness. He said he did not mind what she said; but she saw plainly that he was offended, and in his heart did not forgive her. She did not feel inclined to tell Mahin about her quarrel with her father; as to her sister, she was very cold to Lisa, being jealous of Mahin's love for her.

"I ought to confess to God," she said to herself. As all this happened in Lent, she made up her mind to fast in preparation for the communion, and to reveal all her thoughts to the father confessor, asking his advice as to what she ought to decide for the future.

At a small distance from her town a monastery was situated, where an old monk lived who had gained a great reputation by his holy life, by his sermons and prophecies, as well as by the marvellous cures ascribed to him.

The monk had received a letter from Lisa's father announcing the visit of his daughter, and telling him in what a state of excitement the young girl was. He also expressed the hope in that letter that the monk would influence her in the right way, urging her not to depart from the golden mean, and to live like a good Christian without trying to upset the present conditions of her life.

The monk received Lisa after he had seen many other people, and being very tired, began by quietly recommending her to be modest and to submit to her present conditions of life and to her parents. Lisa listened silently, blushing and flushed with excitement. When he had finished admonishing her, she began saying with tears in her eyes, timidly at first, that Christ bade us leave father and mother to follow Him. Getting more and more excited, she told him her conception of Christ. The monk smiled slightly, and replied as he generally did when admonishing his penitents; but after a while he remained silent, repeating with heavy sighs, "O God!" Then he said, "Well, come to confession to-morrow," and blessed her with his wrinkled hands.

The next day Lisa came to confession, and without renewing their interrupted conversation, he absolved her and refused to dispose of her fortune, giving no reasons for doing so.

Lisa's purity, her devotion to God and her ardent soul, impressed the monk deeply. He had desired long ago to renounce the world entirely; but the brotherhood, which drew a large income from his work as a preacher, insisted on his continuing his activity. He gave way, although he had a vague feeling that he was in a false position. It was rumoured that he was a miracle-working saint, whereas in reality he was a weak man, proud of his success in the world. When the soul of Lisa was revealed to him, he saw clearly into his own soul. He discovered how different he was to what he wanted to be, and realised the desire of his heart.

Soon after Lisa's visit he went to live in a separate cell as a hermit, and for three weeks did not officiate again in the church of the friary. After the celebration of the mass, he preached a sermon denouncing his own sins and those of the world, and urging all to repent.

From that day he preached every fortnight, and his sermons attracted increasing audiences. His fame as a preacher spread abroad. His sermons were extraordinarily fearless and sincere, and deeply impressed all who listened to him.

XII

Vassily was actually carrying out the object he had in leaving the prison. With the help of a few friends he broke into the house of the rich merchant Krasnopuzov, whom he knew to be a miser and a debauchee. Vassily took out of his writing-desk thirty thousand roubles, and began disposing of them as he thought right. He even gave up drink, so as not to spend that money on himself, but to distribute it to the poor; helping poor girls to get married; paying off people's debts, and doing this all without ever revealing himself to those he helped; his only desire was to distribute his money in the right way. As he also gave bribes to the police, he was left in peace for a long time.

His heart was singing for joy. When at last he was arrested and put to trial, he confessed with pride that he had robbed the fat merchant. "The money," he said, "was lying idle in that fool's desk, and he did not even know how much he had, whereas I have put it into circulation and helped a lot of good people."

The counsel for the defence spoke with such good humour and kindness that the jury felt inclined to discharge Vassily, but sentenced him nevertheless to confinement in prison. He thanked the jury, and assured them that he would find his way out of prison before long.

XIII

Natalia Ivanovna Sventizky's telegram proved useless. The committee appointed to deal with the petitions in the Emperor's name, decided not even to make a report to the Czar. But one day when the Sventizky case was discussed at the Emperor's luncheon-table, the chairman of the committee, who was present, mentioned the telegram which had been received from Sventizky's widow.

"C'est tres gentil de sa part," said one of the ladies of the imperial family.

The Emperor sighed, shrugged his shoulders, adorned with epaulettes. "The law," he said; and raised his glass for the groom of the chamber to pour out some Moselle.

All those present pretended to admire the wisdom of the sovereign's words. There was no further question about the telegram. The two peasants, the old man and the young boy, were hanged by a Tartar hangman from Kazan, a cruel convict and a murderer.

The old man's wife wanted to dress the body of her husband in a white shirt, with white bands which serve as stockings, and new boots, but she was not allowed to do so. The two men were buried together in the same pit outside the church-yard wall.

"Princess Sofia Vladimirovna tells me he is a very remarkable preacher," remarked the old Empress, the Emperor's mother, one day to her son: "Faites le venir. Il peut precher a la cathedrale."

"No, it would be better in the palace church," said the Emperor, and ordered the hermit Isidor to be invited.

All the generals, and other high officials, assembled in the church of the imperial palace; it was an event to hear the famous preacher.

A thin and grey old man appeared, looked at those present, and said: "In the name of God, the Son, and the Holy Ghost," and began to speak.

At first all went well, but the longer he spoke the worse it became. "Il devient de plus en plus aggressif," as the Empress put it afterwards. He fulminated against every one. He spoke about the executions and charged the government with having made so many necessary. How can the government of a Christian country kill men?

Everybody looked at everybody else, thinking of the bad taste of the sermon, and how unpleasant it must be for the Emperor to listen to it; but nobody expressed these thoughts aloud.

When Isidor had said Amen, the metropolitan approached, and asked him to call on him.

After Isidor had had a talk with the metropolitan and with the attorney-general, he was immediately sent away to a friary, not his own, but one at Suzdal, which had a prison attached to it; the prior of that friary was now Father Missael.

XIV

Every one tried to look as if Isidor's sermon contained nothing unpleasant, and nobody mentioned it. It seemed to the Czar that the hermit's words had not made any impression on himself; but once or twice during that day he caught himself thinking of the two peasants who had been hanged, and the widow of Sventizky who had asked an amnesty for them. That day the Emperor had to be present at a parade; after which he went out for a drive; a reception of ministers came next, then dinner, after dinner the theatre. As usual, the Czar fell asleep the moment his head touched the pillow. In the night an awful dream awoke him: he saw gallows in a large field and corpses dangling on them; the tongues of the corpses were protruding, and their bodies moved and shook. And somebody shouted, "It is you—you who have done it!" The Czar woke up bathed in perspiration and began to think.

It was the first time that he had ever thought of the responsibilities which weighed on him, and the words of old Isidor came back to his mind. . . .

But only dimly could he see himself as a mere human being, and he could not consider his mere human wants and duties, because of all that was required of him as Czar. As to acknowledging that human duties were more obligatory than those of a Czar—he had not strength for that.

XV

Having served his second term in the prison, Prokofy, who had formerly worked on the Sventizky estate, was no longer the brisk, ambitious, smartly dressed fellow he had been. He seemed, on the contrary, a complete wreck. When sober he would sit idle and would refuse to do any work, however much his father scolded him; moreover, he was continually seeking to get hold of something secretly, and take it to the public-house for a drink. When he came home he would continue to sit idle, coughing and spitting all the time. The doctor on whom he called, examined his chest and shook his head.

"You, my man, ought to have many things which you have not got."

"That is usually the case, isn't it?"

"Take plenty of milk, and don't smoke."

"These are days of fasting, and besides we have no cow."

Once in spring he could not get any sleep; he was longing to have a drink. There was nothing in the house he could lay his hand on to take to the public-house. He put on his cap and went out. He walked along the street up to the house where the priest and the deacon lived together. The deacon's harrow stood outside leaning against the hedge. Prokofy approached, took the harrow upon his shoulder, and walked to an inn kept by a woman, Petrovna. She might give him a small bottle of vodka for it. But he had hardly gone a few steps when the deacon came out of his house. It was already dawn, and he saw that Prokofy was carrying away his harrow.

"Hey, what's that?" cried the deacon.

The neighbours rushed out from their houses. Prokofy was seized, brought to the police station, and then sentenced to eleven months' imprisonment. It was autumn, and Prokofy had to be transferred to the prison hospital. He was coughing badly; his chest was heaving from the exertion; and he could not get warm. Those who were stronger contrived not to shiver; Prokofy on the contrary shivered day and night, as the superintendent would not light the fires in the hospital till November, to save expense.

Prokofy suffered greatly in body, and still more in soul. He was disgusted with his surroundings, and hated every one—the deacon, the superintendent who would not light the fires, the guard, and the man who was lying in the bed next to his, and who had a swollen red lip. He began also to hate the new convict who was brought into hospital. This convict was Stepan. He was suffering from some disease on his head, and was transferred to the hospital and put in a bed at Prokofy's side. After a time that hatred to Stepan changed, and Prokofy became, on the contrary, extremely fond of him; he delighted in talking to him. It was only after a talk with Stepan that his anguish would cease for a while. Stepan always told every one he met about his last murder, and how it had impressed him.

"Far from shrieking, or anything of that kind," he said to Prokofy, "she did not move. 'Kill me! There I am,' she said. 'But it is not my soul you destroy, it is your own.'"

"Well, of course, it is very dreadful to kill. I had one day to slaughter a sheep, and even that made me half mad. I have not destroyed any living soul; why then do those villains kill me? I have done no harm to anybody . . ."

"That will be taken into consideration."

"By whom?"

"By God, to be sure."

"I have not seen anything yet showing that God exists, and I don't believe in Him, brother. I think when a man dies, grass will grow over the spot, and that is the end of it."

"You are wrong to think like that. I have murdered so many people, whereas she, poor soul, was helping everybody. And you think she and I are to have the same lot? Oh no! Only wait."

"Then you believe the soul lives on after a man is dead?"

"To be sure; it truly lives."

Prokofy suffered greatly when death drew near. He could hardly breathe. But in the very last hour he felt suddenly relieved from all pain. He called Stepan to him. "Farewell, brother," he said. "Death has come, I see. I was so afraid of it before. And now I don't mind. I only wish it to come quicker."

XVI

In the meanwhile, the affairs of Eugene Mihailovich had grown worse and worse. Business was very slack. There was a new shop in the town; he was losing his customers, and the interest had to be paid. He borrowed again on interest. At last his shop and his goods were to be sold up. Eugene Mihailovich and his wife applied to every one they knew, but they could not raise the four hundred roubles they needed to save the shop anywhere.

They had some hope of the merchant Krasnopuzov, Eugene Mihailovich's wife being on good terms with his mistress. But news came that Krasnopuzov had been robbed of a huge sum of money. Some said of half a million roubles. "And do you know who is said to be the thief?" said Eugene Mihailovich to his wife. "Vassily, our former yard-porter. They say he is squandering the money, and the police are bribed by him."

"I knew he was a villain. You remember how he did not mind perjuring himself? But I did not expect it would go so far."

"I hear he has recently been in the courtyard of our house. Cook says she is sure it was he. She told me he helps poor girls to get married."

"They always invent tales. I don't believe it."

At that moment a strange man, shabbily dressed, entered the shop.

"What is it you want?"

"Here is a letter for you."

"From whom?"

"You will see yourself."

"Don't you require an answer? Wait a moment."

"I cannot." The strange man handed the letter and disappeared.

"How extraordinary!" said Eugene Mihailovich, and tore open the envelope. To his great amazement several hundred rouble notes fell out. "Four hundred roubles!" he exclaimed, hardly believing his eyes. "What does it mean?"

The envelope also contained a badly-spelt letter, addressed to Eugene Mihailovich. "It is said in the Gospels," ran the letter, "do good for evil. You have done me much harm; and in the coupon case you made me wrong the peasants greatly. But I have pity for you. Here are four hundred notes. Take them, and remember your porter Vassily."

"Very extraordinary!" said Eugene Mihailovich to his wife and to himself. And each time he remembered that incident, or spoke about it to his wife, tears would come to his eyes.

XVII

Fourteen priests were kept in the Suzdal friary prison, chiefly for having been untrue to the orthodox faith. Isidor had been sent to that place also. Father Missael received him according to the instructions he had been given, and without talking to him ordered him to be put into a separate cell as a serious criminal. After a fortnight Father Missael, making a round of the prison, entered Isidor's cell, and asked him whether there was anything he wished for.

"There is a great deal I wish for," answered Isidor; "but I cannot tell you what it is in the presence of anybody else. Let me talk to you privately."

They looked at each other, and Missael saw he had nothing to be afraid of in remaining alone with Isidor. He ordered Isidor to be brought into his own room, and when they were alone, he said,—"Well, now you can speak."

Isidor fell on his knees.

"Brother," said Isidor. "What are you doing to yourself! Have mercy on your own soul. You are the worst villain in the world. You have offended against all that is sacred . . ."

A month after Missael sent a report, asking that Isidor should be released as he had repented, and he also asked for the release of the rest of the prisoners. After which he resigned his post.

XVIII

Ten years passed. Mitia Smokovnikov had finished his studies in the Technical College; he was now an engineer in the gold mines in Siberia, and was very highly paid. One day he was about to make a round in the district. The governor offered him a convict, Stepan Pelageushkine, to accompany him on his journey.

"A convict, you say? But is not that dangerous?"

"Not if it is this one. He is a holy man. You may ask anybody, they will all tell you so."

"Why has he been sent here?"

The governor smiled. "He had committed six murders, and yet he is a holy man. I go bail for him."

Mitia Smokovnikov took Stepan, now a bald-headed, lean, tanned man, with him on his journey. On their way Stepan took care of Smokovnikov, like his own child, and told him his story; told him why he had been sent here, and what now filled his life.

And, strange to say, Mitia Smokovnikov, who up to that time used to spend his time drinking, eating, and gambling, began for the first time to meditate on life. These thoughts never left him now, and produced a complete change in his habits. After a time he was offered a very advantageous position. He refused it, and made up his mind to buy an estate with the money he had, to marry, and to devote himself to the peasantry, helping them as much as he could.

XIX

He carried out his intentions. But before retiring to his estate he called on his father, with whom he had been on bad terms, and who had settled apart with his new family. Mitia Smokovnikov wanted to make it up. The old man wondered at first, and laughed at the change he noticed in his son; but after a while he ceased to find fault with him, and thought of the many times when it was he who was the guilty one.

AFTER THE DANCE

"—AND you say that a man cannot, of himself, understand what is good and evil; that it is all environment, that the environment swamps the man. But I believe it is all chance. Take my own case . . ."

Thus spoke our excellent friend, Ivan Vasilievich, after a conversation between us on the impossibility of improving individual character without a change of the conditions under which men live. Nobody had actually said that one could not of oneself understand good and evil; but it was a habit of Ivan Vasilievich to answer in this way the thoughts aroused in his own mind by conversation, and to illustrate those thoughts by relating incidents in his own life. He often quite forgot the reason for his story in telling it; but he always told it with great sincerity and feeling.

He did so now.

"Take my own case. My whole life was moulded, not by environment, but by something quite different."

"By what, then?" we asked.

"Oh, that is a long story. I should have to tell you about a great many things to make you understand."

"Well, tell us then."

Ivan Vasilievich thought a little, and shook his head.

"My whole life," he said, "was changed in one night, or, rather, morning."

"Why, what happened?" one of us asked.

"What happened was that I was very much in love. I have been in love many times, but this was the most serious of all. It is a thing of the past; she has married daughters now. It was Varinka B—." Ivan Vasilievich mentioned her surname. "Even at fifty she is remarkably handsome; but in her youth, at eighteen, she was exquisite—tall, slender, graceful, and stately. Yes, stately is the word; she held herself very erect, by instinct as it were; and carried her head high, and that together with her beauty and height gave her a queenly air in spite of being thin, even bony one might say. It might indeed have been deterring had it not been for her smile, which was always gay and cordial, and for the charming light in her eyes and for her youthful sweetness."

"What an entrancing description you give, Ivan Vasilievich!"

"Description, indeed! I could not possibly describe her so that you could appreciate her. But that does not matter; what I am going to tell you happened in the forties. I was at that time a student in a provincial university. I don't know whether it was a good thing or no, but we had no political clubs, no theories in our universities then. We were simply young and spent our time as young men do, studying and amusing ourselves. I was a very gay, lively, careless fellow, and had plenty of money too. I had a fine horse, and used to go tobogganing with the young ladies. Skating had not yet come into fashion. I went to drinking parties with my comrades—in those days we drank nothing but champagne—if we had no champagne we drank nothing at all. We never drank vodka, as they do now. Evening parties and balls were my favourite amusements. I danced well, and was not an ugly fellow."

"Come, there is no need to be modest," interrupted a lady near him. "We have seen your photograph. Not ugly, indeed! You were a handsome fellow."

"Handsome, if you like. That does not matter. When my love for her was at its strongest, on the last day of the carnival, I was at a ball at the provincial marshal's, a good-natured old man, rich and hospitable, and a court chamberlain. The guests were welcomed by his wife, who was as good-natured as himself. She was dressed in puce-coloured velvet, and had a diamond diadem on her forehead, and her plump, old white shoulders and bosom were bare like the portraits of Empress Elizabeth, the daughter of Peter the Great.

"It was a delightful ball. It was a splendid room, with a gallery for the orchestra, which was famous at the time, and consisted of serfs belonging to a musical landowner. The refreshments were magnificent, and the champagne flowed in rivers. Though I was fond of champagne I did not drink that night, because without it I was drunk with love. But I made up for it by dancing waltzes and polkas till I was ready to drop—of course, whenever possible, with Varinka. She wore a white dress with a pink sash, white shoes, and white kid gloves, which did not quite reach to her thin pointed elbows. A disgusting engineer named

Anisimov robbed me of the mazurka with her—to this day I cannot forgive him. He asked her for the dance the minute she arrived, while I had driven to the hair-dresser's to get a pair of gloves, and was late. So I did not dance the mazurka with her, but with a German girl to whom I had previously paid a little attention; but I am afraid I did not behave very politely to her that evening. I hardly spoke or looked at her, and saw nothing but the tall, slender figure in a white dress, with a pink sash, a flushed, beaming, dimpled face, and sweet, kind eyes. I was not alone; they were all looking at her with admiration, the men and women alike, although she outshone all of them. They could not help admiring her.

"Although I was not nominally her partner for the mazurka, I did as a matter of fact dance nearly the whole time with her. She always came forward boldly the whole length of the room to pick me out. I flew to meet her without waiting to be chosen, and she thanked me with a smile for my intuition. When I was brought up to her with somebody else, and she guessed wrongly, she took the other man's hand with a shrug of her slim shoulders, and smiled at me regretfully.

"Whenever there was a waltz figure in the mazurka, I waltzed with her for a long time, and breathing fast and smiling, she would say, 'Encore'; and I went on waltzing and waltzing, as though unconscious of any bodily existence."

"Come now, how could you be unconscious of it with your arm round her waist? You must have been conscious, not only of your own existence, but of hers," said one of the party.

Ivan Vasilievich cried out, almost shouting in anger: "There you are, moderns all over! Nowadays you think of nothing but the body. It was different in our day. The more I was in love the less corporeal was she in my eyes. Nowadays you think of nothing but the body. It was different in our day. The more I was in love the less corporeal was she in my eyes. Nowadays you set legs, ankles, and I don't know what. You undress the women you are in love with. In my eyes, as Alphonse Karr said—and he was a good writer—' the one I loved was always draped in robes of bronze.' We never thought of doing so; we tried to veil her nakedness, like Noah's good-natured son. Oh, well, you can't understand."

"Don't pay any attention to him. Go on," said one of them.

"Well, I danced for the most part with her, and did not notice how time was passing. The musicians kept playing the same mazurka tunes over and over again in desperate exhaustion—you know what it is towards the end of a ball. Papas and mammas were already getting up from the card-tables in the drawing-room in expectation of supper, the men-servants were running to and fro bringing in things. It was nearly three o'clock. I had to make the most of the last minutes. I chose her again for the mazurka, and for the hundredth time we danced across the room.

"'The quadrille after supper is mine,' I said, taking her to her place.

"'Of course, if I am not carried off home,' she said, with a smile.

"'I won't give you up,' I said.

"'Give me my fan, anyhow,' she answered.

"'I am so sorry to part with it,' I said, handing her a cheap white fan.

"'Well, here's something to console you,' she said, plucking a feather out of the fan, and giving it to me.

"I took the feather, and could only express my rapture and gratitude with my eyes. I was not only pleased and gay, I was happy, delighted; I was good, I was not myself but some being not of this earth, knowing nothing of evil. I hid the feather in my glove, and stood there unable to tear myself away from her.

"'Look, they are urging father to dance,' she said to me, pointing to the tall, stately figure of her father, a colonel with silver epaulettes, who was standing in the doorway with some ladies.

"'Varinka, come here!' exclaimed our hostess, the lady with the diamond ferronniere and with shoulders like Elizabeth, in a loud voice.

"'Varinka went to the door, and I followed her.

"'Persuade your father to dance the mazurka with you, ma chere.—Do, please, Peter Valdislavovich,' she said, turning to the colonel.

"'Varinka's father was a very handsome, well-preserved old man. He had a good colour, moustaches curled in the style of Nicolas I., and white whiskers which met the moustaches. His hair was combed on to his forehead, and a bright smile, like his daughter's, was on his lips and in his eyes. He was splendidly set up, with a broad military chest, on which he wore some decorations, and he had powerful shoulders and long slim legs. He was that ultra-military type produced by the discipline of Emperor Nicolas I.

"'When we approached the door the colonel was just refusing to dance, saying that he had quite forgotten how; but at that instant he smiled, swung his arm gracefully around to the left, drew his sword from its sheath, handed it to an obliging young man who stood near, and smoothed his suede glove on his right hand.

"'Everything must be done according to rule,' he said with a smile. He took the hand of his daughter, and stood one-quarter turned, waiting for the music.

"At the first sound of the mazurka, he stamped one foot smartly, threw the other forward, and, at first slowly and smoothly, then buoyantly and impetuously, with stamping of feet and clicking of boots, his tall, imposing figure moved the length of the room. Varinka swayed gracefully beside him, rhythmically and easily, making her steps short or long, with her little feet in their white satin slippers.

"All the people in the room followed every movement of the couple. As for me I not only admired, I regarded them with enraptured sympathy. I was particularly impressed with the old gentleman's boots. They were not the modern pointed affairs, but were made of cheap leather, squared-toed, and evidently built by the regimental cobbler. In order that his daughter might dress and go out in society, he did not buy fashionable boots, but wore home-made ones, I thought, and his square toes seemed to me most touching. It was obvious that in his time he had been a good dancer; but now he was too heavy, and his legs had not spring enough for all the beautiful steps he tried to take. Still, he contrived to go twice round the room. When at the end, standing with legs apart, he suddenly clicked his feet together and fell on one knee, a bit heavily, and she danced gracefully around him, smiling and adjusting her skirt, the whole room applauded.

"Rising with an effort, he tenderly took his daughter's face between his hands. He kissed her on the forehead, and brought her to me, under the impression that I was her partner for the mazurka. I said I was not. 'Well, never mind, just go around the room once with her,' he said, smiling kindly, as he replaced his sword in the sheath.

"As the contents of a bottle flow readily when the first drop has been poured, so my love for Varinka seemed to set free the whole force of loving within me. In surrounding her it embraced the world. I loved the hostess with her diadem and her shoulders like Elizabeth, and her husband and her guests and her footmen, and even the engineer Anisimov who felt peevish towards me. As for Varinka's father, with his home-made boots and his kind smile, so like her own, I felt a sort of tenderness for him that was almost rapture.

"After supper I danced the promised quadrille with her, and though I had been infinitely happy before, I grew still happier every moment.

"We did not speak of love. I neither asked myself nor her whether she loved me. It was quite enough to know that I loved her. And I had only one fear—that something might come to interfere with my great joy.

"When I went home, and began to undress for the night, I found it quite out of the question. I held the little feather out of her fan in my hand, and one of her gloves which she gave me when I helped her into the carriage after her mother. Looking at these things, and without closing my eyes I could see her before me as she was for an instant when she had to choose between two partners. She tried to guess what kind of person was represented in me, and I could hear her sweet voice as she said, 'Pride—am I right?' and merrily gave me her hand. At supper she took the first sip from my glass of champagne, looking at me over the rim with her caressing glance. But, plainest of all, I could see her as she danced with her father, gliding along beside him, and looking at the admiring observers with pride and happiness.

"He and she were united in my mind in one rush of pathetic tenderness.

"I was living then with my brother, who has since died. He disliked going out, and never went to dances; and besides, he was busy preparing for his last university examinations, and was leading a very regular life. He was asleep. I looked at him, his head buried in the pillow and half covered with the quilt; and I affectionately pitied him, pitied him for his ignorance of the bliss I was experiencing. Our serf Petrusha had met me with a candle, ready to undress me, but I sent him away. His sleepy face and tousled hair seemed to me so touching. Trying not to make a noise, I went to my room on tiptoe and sat down on my bed. No, I was too happy; I could not sleep. Besides, it was too hot in the rooms. Without taking off my uniform, I went quietly into the hall, put on my overcoat, opened the front door and stepped out into the street.

"It was after four when I had left the ball; going home and stopping there a while had occupied two hours, so by the time I went out it was dawn. It was regular carnival weather—foggy, and the road full of water-soaked snow just melting, and water dripping from the eaves. Varinka's family lived on the edge of town near a large field, one end of which was a parade ground: at the other end was a boarding-school for young ladies. I passed through our empty little street and came to the main thoroughfare, where I met pedestrians and sledges laden with wood, the runners grating the road. The horses swung with regular paces beneath their shining yokes, their backs covered with straw mats and their heads wet with rain; while the drivers, in enormous boots, splashed through the mud beside the sledges. All this, the very horses themselves, seemed to me stimulating and fascinating, full of suggestion.

"When I approached the field near their house, I saw at one end of it, in the direction of the parade ground, something very huge and black, and I heard sounds of fife and drum proceeding from it. My heart had been full of song, and I had heard in imagination the tune of the mazurka, but this was very harsh music. It was not pleasant.

"'What can that be?' I thought, and went towards the sound by a slippery path through the centre of the field. Walking about a hundred paces, I began to distinguish many black objects through the mist. They were evidently soldiers. 'It is probably a drill,' I thought.

"So I went along in that direction in company with a blacksmith, who wore a dirty coat and an apron, and was carrying something. He walked ahead of me as we approached the place. The soldiers in black uniforms stood in two rows, facing each other motionless, their guns at rest. Behind them stood the fifes and drums, incessantly repeating the same unpleasant tune.

"'What are they doing?' I asked the blacksmith, who halted at my side.

"'A Tartar is being beaten through the ranks for his attempt to desert,' said the blacksmith in an angry tone, as he looked intently at the far end of the line.

"I looked in the same direction, and saw between the files something horrid approaching me. The thing that approached was a man, stripped to the waist, fastened with cords to the guns of two soldiers who were leading him. At his side an officer in overcoat and cap was walking, whose figure had a familiar look. The victim advanced under the blows that rained upon him from both sides, his whole body plunging, his feet dragging through the snow. Now he threw himself backward, and the subalterns who led him thrust him forward. Now he fell forward, and they pulled him up short; while ever at his side marched the tall officer, with firm and nervous pace. It was Varinka's father, with his rosy face and white moustache.

"At each stroke the man, as if amazed, turned his face, grimacing with pain, towards the side whence the blow came, and showing his white teeth repeated the same words over and over. But I could only hear what the words were when he came quite near. He did not speak them, he sobbed them out,—"Brothers, have mercy on me! Brothers, have mercy on me!' But the brothers had, no mercy, and when the procession came close to me, I saw how a soldier who stood opposite me took a firm step forward and lifting his stick with a whirr, brought it down upon the man's back. The man plunged forward, but the subalterns pulled him back, and another blow came down from the other side, then from this side and then from the other. The colonel marched beside him, and looking now at his feet and now at the man, inhaled the air, puffed out his cheeks, and breathed it out between his protruded lips. When they passed the place where I stood, I caught a glimpse between the two files of the back of the man that was being punished. It was something so many-coloured, wet, red, unnatural, that I could hardly believe it was a human body.

"'My God!'" muttered the blacksmith.

The procession moved farther away. The blows continued to rain upon the writhing, falling creature; the fifes shrilled and the drums beat, and the tall imposing figure of the colonel moved along-side the man, just as before. Then, suddenly, the colonel stopped, and rapidly approached a man in the ranks.

"'I'll teach you to hit him gently,' I heard his furious voice say. 'Will you pat him like that? Will you?' and I saw how his strong hand in the suede glove struck the weak, bloodless, terrified soldier for not bringing down his stick with sufficient strength on the red neck of the Tartar.

"'Bring new sticks!' he cried, and looking round, he saw me. Assuming an air of not knowing me, and with a ferocious, angry frown, he hastily turned away. I felt so utterly ashamed that I didn't know where to look. It was as if I had been detected in a disgraceful act. I dropped my eyes, and quickly hurried home. All the way I had the drums beating and the fifes whistling in my ears. And I heard the words, 'Brothers, have mercy on me!' or 'Will you pat him? Will you?' My heart was full of physical disgust that was almost sickness. So much so that I halted several times on my way, for I had the feeling that I was going to be really sick from all the horrors that possessed me at that sight. I do not remember how I got home and got to bed. But the moment I was about to fall asleep I heard and saw again all that had happened, and I sprang up.

"'Evidently he knows something I do not know,' I thought about the colonel. 'If I knew what he knows I should certainly grasp—understand—what I have just seen, and it would not cause me such suffering.'

"But however much I thought about it, I could not understand the thing that the colonel knew. It was evening before I could get to sleep, and then only after calling on a friend and drinking till I; was quite drunk.

"Do you think I had come to the conclusion that the deed I had witnessed was wicked? Oh, no. Since it was done with such assurance, and was recognised by every one as indispensable, they doubtless knew something which I did not know. So I thought, and tried to understand. But no matter, I could never understand it, then or afterwards. And not being able to grasp it, I could not enter the service as I had intended. I don't mean only the military service: I did not enter the Civil Service either. And so I have been of no use whatever, as you can see."

"Yes, we know how useless you've been," said one of us. "Tell us, rather, how many people would be of any use at all if it hadn't been for you."

"Oh, that's utter nonsense," said Ivan Vasilievich, with genuine annoyance.

"Well; and what about the love affair?

"My love? It decreased from that day. When, as often happened, she looked dreamy and meditative, I instantly recollected the colonel on the parade ground, and I felt so awkward and uncomfortable that I began to see her less frequently. So my love came to naught. Yes; such chances arise, and they alter and direct a man's whole life," he said in summing up. "And you say . . ."

Alyosha the Pot

ALYOSHA was the younger brother. He was called the Pot, because his mother had once sent him with a pot of milk to the deacon's wife, and he had stumbled against something and broken it. His mother had beaten him, and the children had teased him. Since then he was nicknamed the Pot. Alyosha was a tiny, thin little fellow, with ears like wings, and a huge nose. "Alyosha has a nose that looks like a dog on a hill!" the children used to call after him. Alyosha went to the village school, but was not good at lessons; besides, there was so little time to learn. His elder brother was in town, working for a merchant, so Alyosha had to help his father from a very early age. When he was no more than six he used to go out with the girls to watch the cows and sheep in the pasture, and a little later he looked after the horses by day and by night. And at twelve years of age he had already begun to plough and to drive the cart. The skill was there though the strength was not. He was always cheerful. Whenever the children made fun of him, he would either laugh or be silent. When his father scolded him he would stand mute and listen attentively, and as soon as the scolding was over would smile and go on with his work. Alyosha was nineteen when his brother was taken as a soldier. So his father placed him with the merchant as a yard-porter. He was given his brother's old boots, his father's old coat and cap, and was taken to town. Alyosha was delighted with his clothes, but the merchant was not impressed by his appearance.

"I thought you would bring me a man in Simeon's place," he said, scanning Alyosha; "and you've brought me *this!* What's the good of him?"

"He can do everything; look after horses and drive. He's a good one to work. He looks rather thin, but he's tough enough. And he's very willing."

"He looks it. All right; we'll see what we can do with him."

So Alyosha remained at the merchant's.

The family was not a large one. It consisted of the merchant's wife: her old mother: a married son poorly educated who was in his father's business: another son, a learned one who had finished school and entered the University, but having been expelled, was living at home: and a daughter who still went to school.

They did not take to Alyosha at first. He was uncouth, badly dressed, and had no manner, but they soon got used to him. Alyosha worked even better than his brother had done; he was really very willing. They sent him on all sorts of errands, but he did everything quickly and readily, going from one task to another without stopping. And so here, just as at home, all the work was put upon his shoulders. The more he did, the more he was given to do. His mistress, her old mother, the son, the daughter, the clerk, and the cook—all ordered him about, and sent him from one place to another.

"Alyosha, do this! Alyosha, do that! What! have you forgotten, Alyosha? Mind you don't forget, Alyosha!" was heard from morning till night. And Alyosha ran here, looked after this and that, forgot nothing, found time for everything, and was always cheerful.

His brother's old boots were soon worn out, and his master scolded him for going about in tatters with his toes sticking out. He ordered another pair to be bought for him in the market. Alyosha was delighted with his new boots, but was angry with his feet when they ached at the end of the day after so much running about. And then he was afraid that his father would be annoyed when he came to town for his wages, to find that his master had deducted the cost of the boots.

In the winter Alyosha used to get up before daybreak. He would chop the wood, sweep the yard, feed the cows and horses, light the stoves, clean the boots, prepare the samovars and polish them afterwards; or the clerk would get him to bring up the goods; or the cook would set him to knead the bread and clean the saucepans. Then he was sent to town on various errands, to bring the daughter home from school, or to get some olive oil for the old mother. "Why the devil have you been so long?" first one, then another, would say to him. Why should they go? Alyosha can go. "Alyosha! Alyosha!" And Alyosha ran here and there. He breakfasted in snatches while he was working, and rarely managed to get his dinner at the proper hour. The cook used to scold him for being late, but she was sorry for him all the same, and would keep something hot for his dinner and supper.

At holiday times there was more work than ever, but Alyosha liked holidays because everybody gave him a tip. Not much certainly, but it would amount up to about sixty kopeks [1s 2d]—his very own money. For Alyosha never set eyes on his wages. His father used to come and take them from the merchant, and only scold Alyosha for wearing out his boots.

When he had saved up two roubles [4s], by the advice of the cook he bought himself a red knitted jacket, and was so happy when he put it on, that he couldn't close his mouth for joy. Alyosha was not talkative; when he spoke at all, he spoke abruptly, with his head turned away. When told to do anything, or asked if he could do it, he would say yes without the smallest hesitation, and set to work at once.

Alyosha did not know any prayer; and had forgotten what his mother had taught him. But he prayed just the same, every morning and every evening, prayed with his hands, crossing himself.

He lived like this for about a year and a half, and towards the end of the second year a most startling thing happened to him. He discovered one day, to his great surprise, that, in addition to the relation of usefulness existing between people, there was also another, a peculiar relation of quite a different character. Instead of a man being wanted to clean boots, and go on errands and harness horses, he is not wanted to be of any service at all, but another human being wants to serve him and pet him. Suddenly Alyosha felt he was such a man.

He made this discovery through the cook Ustinia. She was young, had no parents, and worked as hard as Alyosha. He felt for the first time in his life that he—not his services, but he himself—was necessary to another human being. When his mother used to be sorry for him, he had taken no notice of her. It had seemed to him quite natural, as though he were feeling sorry for himself. But here was Ustinia, a perfect stranger, and sorry for him. She would save him some hot porridge, and sit watching him, her chin propped on her bare arm, with the sleeve rolled up, while he was eating it. When he looked at her she would begin to laugh, and he would laugh too.

This was such a new, strange thing to him that it frightened Alyosha. He feared that it might interfere with his work. But he was pleased, nevertheless, and when he glanced at the trousers that Ustinia had mended for him, he would shake his head and smile. He would often think of her while at work, or when running on errands. "A fine girl, Ustinia!" he sometimes exclaimed.

Ustinia used to help him whenever she could, and he helped her. She told him all about her life; how she had lost her parents; how her aunt had taken her in and found a place for her in the town; how the merchant's son had tried to take liberties with her, and how she had rebuffed him. She liked to talk, and Alyosha liked to listen to her. He had heard that peasants who came up to work in the towns frequently got married to servant girls. On one occasion she asked him if his parents intended marrying him soon. He said that he did not know; that he did not want to marry any of the village girls.

"Have you taken a fancy to some one, then?"

"I would marry you, if you'd be willing."

"Get along with you, Alyosha the Pot; but you've found your tongue, haven't you?" she exclaimed, slapping him on the back with a towel she held in her hand. "Why shouldn't I?"

At Shrovetide Alyosha's father came to town for his wages. It had come to the ears of the merchant's wife that Alyosha wanted to marry Ustinia, and she disapproved of it. "What will be the use of her with a baby?" she thought, and informed her husband.

The merchant gave the old man Alyosha's wages.

"How is my lad getting on?" he asked. "I told you he was willing."

"That's all right, as far as it goes, but he's taken some sort of nonsense into his head. He wants to marry our cook. Now I don't approve of married servants. We won't have them in the house."

"Well, now, who would have thought the fool would think of such a thing?" the old man exclaimed. "But don't you worry. I'll soon settle that."

He went into the kitchen, and sat down at the table waiting for his son. Alyosha was out on an errand, and came back breathless.

"I thought you had some sense in you; but what's this you've taken into your head?" his father began.

"I? Nothing."

"How, nothing? They tell me you want to get married. You shall get married when the time comes. I'll find you a decent wife, not some town hussy."

His father talked and talked, while Alyosha stood still and sighed. When his father had quite finished, Alyosha smiled.

"All right. I'll drop it."

"Now that's what I call sense."

When he was left alone with Ustinia he told her what his father had said. (She had listened at the door.)

"It's no good; it can't come off. Did you hear? He was angry—won't have it at any price."

Ustinia cried into her apron.

Alyosha shook his head.

"What's to be done? We must do as we're told."

"Well, are you going to give up that nonsense, as your father told you?" his mistress asked, as he was putting up the shutters in the evening.

"To be sure we are," Alyosha replied with a smile, and then burst into tears.

From that day Alyosha went about his work as usual, and no longer talked to Ustinia about their getting married. One day in Lent the clerk told him to clear the snow from the roof. Alyosha climbed on to the roof and swept away all the snow; and, while he was still raking out some frozen lumps from the gutter, his foot slipped and he fell over. Unfortunately he did not fall on the snow, but on a piece of iron over the door. Ustinia came running up, together with the merchant's daughter.

"Have you hurt yourself, Alyosha?"

"Ah! no, it's nothing."

But he could not raise himself when he tried to, and began to smile.

He was taken into the lodge. The doctor arrived, examined him, and asked where he felt the pain.

"I feel it all over," he said. "But it doesn't matter. I'm only afraid master will be annoyed. Father ought to be told."

Alyosha lay in bed for two days, and on the third day they sent for the priest.

"Are you really going to die?" Ustinia asked.

"Of course I am. You can't go on living for ever. You must go when the time comes." Alyosha spoke rapidly as usual. "Thank you, Ustinia. You've been very good to me. What a lucky thing they didn't let us marry! Where should we have been now? It's much better as it is."

When the priest came, he prayed with his bands and with his heart. "As it is good here when you obey and do no harm to others, so it will be there," was the thought within it.

He spoke very little; he only said he was thirsty, and he seemed full of wonder at something.

He lay in wonderment, then stretched himself, and died.

MY DREAM

"**As** a daughter she no longer exists for me. Can't you understand? She simply doesn't exist. Still, I cannot possibly leave her to the charity of strangers. I will arrange things so that she can live as she pleases, but I do not wish to hear of her. Who would ever have thought . . . the horror of it, the horror of it."

He shrugged his shoulders, shook his head, and raised his eyes. These words were spoken by Prince Michael Ivanovich to his brother Peter, who was governor of a province in Central Russia. Prince Peter was a man of fifty, Michael's junior by ten years.

On discovering that his daughter, who had left his house a year before, had settled here with her child, the elder brother had come from St. Petersburg to the provincial town, where the above conversation took place.

Prince Michael Ivanovich was a tall, handsome, white-haired, fresh coloured man, proud and attractive in appearance and bearing. His family consisted of a vulgar, irritable wife, who wrangled with him continually over every petty detail, a son, a ne'er-do-well, spendthrift and roue—yet a "gentleman," according to his father's code, two daughters, of whom the elder had married well, and was living in St. Petersburg; and the younger, Lisa—his favourite, who had disappeared from home a year before. Only a short while ago he had found her with her child in this provincial town.

Prince Peter wanted to ask his brother how, and under what circumstances, Lisa had left home, and who could possibly be the father of her child. But he could not make up his mind to inquire.

That very morning, when his wife had attempted to condole with her brother-in-law, Prince Peter had observed a look of pain on his brother's face. The look had at once been masked by an expression of unapproachable pride, and he had begun to question her about their flat, and the price she paid. At luncheon, before the family and guests, he had been witty and sarcastic as usual. Towards every one, excepting the children, whom he treated with almost reverent tenderness, he adopted an attitude of distant hauteur. And yet it was so natural to him that every one somehow acknowledged his right to be haughty.

In the evening his brother arranged a game of whist. When he retired to the room which had been made ready for him, and was just beginning to take out his artificial teeth, some one tapped lightly on the door with two fingers.

"Who is that?"

"C'est moi, Michael."

Prince Michael Ivanovich recognised the voice of his sister-in-law, frowned, replaced his teeth, and said to himself, "What does she want?" Aloud he said, "Entrez."

His sister-in-law was a quiet, gentle creature, who bowed in submission to her husband's will. But to many she seemed a crank, and some did not hesitate to call her a fool. She was pretty, but her hair was always carelessly dressed, and she herself was untidy and absent-minded. She had, also, the strangest, most unaristocratic ideas, by no means fitting in the wife of a high official. These ideas she would express most unexpectedly, to everybody's astonishment, her husband's no less than her friends'.

"Fous pouvez me renvoyer, mais je ne m'en irai pas, je vous le dis d'avance," she began, in her characteristic, indifferent way.

"Dieu preserve," answered her brother-in-law, with his usual somewhat exaggerated politeness, and brought forward a chair for her.

"Ca ne vous derange pas?" she asked, taking out a cigarette. "I'm not going to say anything unpleasant, Michael. I only wanted to say something about Lisochka."

Michael Ivanovich sighed—the word pained him; but mastering himself at once, he answered with a tired smile. "Our conversation can only be on one subject, and that is the subject you wish to discuss." He spoke without looking at her, and avoided even naming the subject. But his plump, pretty little sister-in-law was unabashed. She continued to regard him with the same gentle, imploring look in her blue eyes, sighing even more deeply.

"Michael, mon bon ami, have pity on her. She is only human."

"I never doubted that," said Michael Ivanovich with a bitter smile.

"She is your daughter."

"She was—but my dear Aline, why talk about this?"

"Michael, dear, won't you see her? I only wanted to say, that the one who is to blame—"

Prince Michael Ivanovich flushed; his face became cruel.

"For heaven's sake, let us stop. I have suffered enough. I have now but one desire, and that is to put her in such a position that she will be independent of others, and that she shall have no further need of communicating with me. Then she can live her own life, and my family and I need know nothing more about her. That is all I can do."

"Michael, you say nothing but 'I'! She, too, is 'I.'"

"No doubt; but, dear Aline, please let us drop the matter. I feel it too deeply."

Alexandra Dmitrievna remained silent for a few moments, shaking her head. "And Masha, your wife, thinks as you do?"

"Yes, quite."

Alexandra Dmitrievna made an inarticulate sound.

"Brisons la dessus et bonne nuit," said he. But she did not go. She stood silent a moment. Then,—"Peter tells me you intend to leave the money with the woman where she lives. Have you the address?"

"I have."

"Don't leave it with the woman, Michael! Go yourself. Just see how she lives. If you don't want to see her, you need not. HE isn't there; there is no one there."

Michael Ivanovich shuddered violently.

"Why do you torture me so? It's a sin against hospitality!"

Alexandra Dmitrievna rose, and almost in tears, being touched by her own pleading, said, "She is so miserable, but she is such a dear."

He got up, and stood waiting for her to finish. She held out her hand.

"Michael, you do wrong," said she, and left him.

For a long while after she had gone Michael Ivanovich walked to and fro on the square of carpet. He frowned and shivered, and exclaimed, "Oh, oh!" And then the sound of his own voice frightened him, and he was silent.

His wounded pride tortured him. His daughter—his—brought up in the house of her mother, the famous Avdotia Borisovna, whom the Empress honoured with her visits, and acquaintance with whom was an honour for all the world! His daughter—; and he had lived his life as a knight of old, knowing neither fear nor blame. The fact that he had a natural son born of a Frenchwoman, whom he had settled abroad, did not lower his own self-esteem. And now this daughter, for whom he had not only done everything that a father could and should do; this daughter to whom he had given a splendid education and every opportunity to make a match in the best Russian society—this daughter to whom he had not only given all that a girl could desire, but whom he had really *loved;* whom he had admired, been proud of—this daughter had repaid him with such disgrace, that he was ashamed and could not face the eyes of men!

He recalled the time when she was not merely his child, and a member of his family, but his darling, his joy and his pride. He saw her again, a little thing of eight or nine, bright, intelligent, lively, impetuous, graceful, with brilliant black eyes and flowing auburn hair. He remembered how she used to jump up on his knees and hug him, and tickle his neck; and how she would laugh, regardless of his protests, and continue to tickle him, and kiss his lips, his eyes, and his cheeks. He was naturally opposed to all demonstration, but this impetuous love moved him, and he often submitted to her petting. He remembered also how sweet it was to caress her. To remember all this, when that sweet child had become what she now was, a creature of whom he could not think without loathing.

He also recalled the time when she was growing into womanhood, and the curious feeling of fear and anger that he experienced when he became aware that men regarded her as a woman. He thought of his jealous love when she came coquettishly to him dressed for a ball, and knowing that she was pretty. He dreaded the passionate glances which fell upon her, that she not only did not understand but rejoiced in. "Yes," thought he, "that superstition of woman's purity! Quite the contrary, they do not know shame—they lack this sense." He remembered how, quite inexplicably to him, she had refused two very good suitors. She had become more and more fascinated by her own success in the round of gaieties she lived in.

But this success could not last long. A year passed, then two, then three. She was a familiar figure, beautiful—but her first youth had passed, and she had become somehow part of the ball-room furniture. Michael Ivanovich remembered how he had realised that she was on the road to spinsterhood, and desired but one thing for her. He must get her married off as quickly as possible, perhaps not quite so well as might have been arranged earlier, but still a respectable match.

But it seemed to him she had behaved with a pride that bordered on insolence. Remembering this, his anger rose more and more fiercely against her. To think of her refusing so many decent men, only to end in this disgrace. "Oh, oh!" he groaned again.

Then stopping, he lit a cigarette, and tried to think of other things. He would send her money, without ever letting her see him. But memories came again. He remembered—it was not so very long ago, for she was more than twenty then—her beginning a flirtation with a boy of fourteen, a cadet of the Corps of Pages who had been staying with them in the country. She had driven the boy half crazy; he had wept in his distraction. Then how she had rebuked her father severely, coldly, and even rudely, when, to put an end to this stupid affair, he had sent the boy away. She seemed somehow to consider herself insulted. Since then father and daughter had drifted into undisguised hostility.

"I was right," he said to himself. "She is a wicked and shameless woman."

And then, as a last ghastly memory, there was the letter from Moscow, in which she wrote that she could not return home; that she was a miserable, abandoned woman, asking only to be forgiven and forgotten. Then the horrid recollection of the scene with his wife came to him; their surmises and their suspicions, which became a certainty. The calamity had happened in Finland, where they had let her visit her aunt; and the culprit was an insignificant Swede, a student, an empty-headed, worthless creature—and married.

All this came back to him now as he paced backwards and forwards on the bedroom carpet, recollecting his former love for her, his pride in her. He recoiled with terror before the incomprehensible fact of her downfall, and he hated her for the agony she was causing him. He remembered the conversation with his sister-in-law, and tried to imagine how he might forgive her. But as soon as the thought of "him" arose, there surged up in his heart horror, disgust, and wounded pride. He groaned aloud, and tried to think of something else.

"No, it is impossible; I will hand over the money to Peter to give her monthly. And as for me, I have no longer a daughter."

And again a curious feeling overpowered him: a mixture of self-pity at the recollection of his love for her, and of fury against her for causing him this anguish.

II

During the last year Lisa had without doubt lived through more than in all the preceding twenty-five. Suddenly she had realised the emptiness of her whole life. It rose before her, base and sordid—this life at home and among the rich set in St. Petersburg—this animal existence that never sounded the depths, but only touched the shallows of life.

It was well enough for a year or two, or perhaps even three. But when it went on for seven or eight years, with its parties, balls, concerts, and suppers; with its costumes and coiffures to display the charms of the body; with its adorers old and young, all alike seemingly possessed of some unaccountable right to have everything, to laugh at everything; and with its summer months spent in the same way, everything yielding but a superficial pleasure, even music and reading merely touching upon life's problems, but never solving them—all this holding out no promise of change, and losing its charm more and more—she began to despair. She had desperate moods when she longed to die.

Her friends directed her thoughts to charity. On the one hand, she saw poverty which was real and repulsive, and a sham poverty even more repulsive and pitiable; on the other, she saw the terrible indifference of the lady patronesses who came in carriages and gowns worth thousands. Life became to her more and more unbearable. She yearned for something real, for life itself—not this playing at living, not this skimming life of its cream. Of real life there was none. The best of her memories was her love for the little cadet Koko. That had been a good, honest, straight-forward impulse, and now there was nothing like it. There could not be. She grew more and more depressed, and in this gloomy mood she went to visit an aunt in Finland. The fresh scenery and surroundings, the people strangely different to her own, appealed to her at any rate as a new experience.

How and when it all began she could not clearly remember. Her aunt had another guest, a Swede. He talked of his work, his people, the latest Swedish novel. Somehow, she herself did not know how that terrible fascination of glances and smiles began, the meaning of which cannot be put into words.

These smiles and glances seemed to reveal to each, not only the soul of the other, but some vital and universal mystery. Every word they spoke was invested by these smiles with a profound and wonderful significance. Music, too, when they were listening together, or when they sang duets, became full of the same deep meaning. So, also, the words in the books they read aloud. Sometimes they would argue, but the moment their eyes met, or a smile flashed between them, the discussion remained far behind. They soared beyond it to some higher plane consecrated to themselves.

How it had come about, how and when the devil, who had seized hold of them both, first appeared behind these smiles and glances, she could not say. But, when terror first seized her, the invisible threads that bound them were already so interwoven that she had no power to tear herself free. She could only count on him and on his honour. She hoped that he would not make use of his power; yet all the while she vaguely desired it.

Her weakness was the greater, because she had nothing to support her in the struggle. She was weary of society life and she had no affection for her mother. Her father, so she thought, had cast her away from him, and she longed passionately to live and to have done with play. Love, the perfect love of a woman for a man, held the promise of life for her. Her strong, passionate nature, too, was dragging her thither. In the tall, strong figure of this man, with his fair hair and light upturned moustache, under which shone a smile attractive and compelling, she saw the promise of that life for which she longed. And then the smiles and glances, the hope of something so incredibly beautiful, led, as they were bound to lead, to that which she feared but unconsciously awaited.

Suddenly all that was beautiful, joyous, spiritual, and full of promise for the future, became animal and sordid, sad and despairing.

She looked into his eyes and tried to smile, pretending that she feared nothing, that everything was as it should be; but deep down in her soul she knew it was all over. She understood that she had not found in him what she had sought; that which she had once known in herself and in Koko. She told him that he must write to her father asking her hand in marriage. This he promised to do; but when she met him next he said it was impossible for him to write just then. She saw something vague and furtive in his eyes, and her distrust of him grew. The following day he wrote to her, telling her that he was already married, though his wife had left him long since; that he knew she would despise him for the wrong he had done her, and implored her forgiveness. She made him come to see her. She said she loved him; that she felt herself bound to him for ever whether he was married or not, and would never leave him. The next time they met he told her that he and his parents were so poor that he could only offer her the meanest existence. She answered that she needed nothing, and was ready to go with him at once wherever he wished. He endeavoured to dissuade her, advising her to wait; and so she waited. But to live on with this secret, with occasional meetings, and merely corresponding with him, all hidden from her family, was agonising, and she insisted again that he must take her away. At first, when she returned to St. Petersburg, he wrote promising to come, and then letters ceased and she knew no more of him.

She tried to lead her old life, but it was impossible. She fell ill, and the efforts of the doctors were unavailing; in her hopelessness she resolved to kill herself. But how was she to do this, so that her death might seem natural? She really desired to take her life, and imagined that she had irrevocably decided on the step. So, obtaining some poison, she poured it into a glass, and in another instant would have drunk it, had not her sister's little son of five at that very moment run in to show her a toy his grandmother had given him. She caressed the child, and, suddenly stopping short, burst into tears.

The thought overpowered her that she, too, might have been a mother had he not been married, and this vision of motherhood made her look into her own soul for the first time. She began to think not of what others would say of her, but of her own life. To kill oneself because of what the world might say was easy; but the moment she saw her own life dissociated from the world, to take that life was out of the question. She threw away the poison, and ceased to think of suicide.

Then her life within began. It was real life, and despite the torture of it, had the possibility been given her, she would not have turned back from it. She began to pray, but there was no comfort in prayer; and her suffering was less for herself than for her father, whose grief she foresaw and understood.

Thus months dragged along, and then something happened which entirely transformed her life. One day, when she was at work upon a quilt, she suddenly experienced a strange sensation. No—it seemed impossible. Motionless she sat with her work in hand. Was it possible that this was *it*. Forgetting everything, his baseness and deceit, her mother's querulousness, and her father's sorrow, she smiled. She shuddered at the recollection that she was on the point of killing it, together with herself.

She now directed all her thoughts to getting away—somewhere where she could bear her child—and become a miserable, pitiful mother, but a mother withal. Somehow she planned and arranged it all, leaving her home and settling in a distant provincial town, where no one could find her, and where she thought she would be far from her people. But, unfortunately, her father's brother received an appointment there, a thing she could not possibly foresee. For four months she had been living in the house of a midwife—one Maria Ivanovna; and, on learning that her uncle had come to the town, she was preparing to fly to a still remoter hiding-place.

III

Michael Ivanovich awoke early next morning. He entered his brother's study, and handed him the cheque, filled in for a sum which he asked him to pay in monthly instalments to his daughter. He inquired when the express left for St. Petersburg. The train left at seven in the evening, giving him time for an early dinner before leaving. He breakfasted with his sister-in-law, who refrained from mentioning the subject which was so painful to him, but only looked at him timidly; and after breakfast he went out for his regular morning walk.

Alexandra Dmitrievna followed him into the hall.

"Go into the public gardens, Michael—it is very charming there, and quite near to Everything," said she, meeting his sombre looks with a pathetic glance.

Michael Ivanovich followed her advice and went to the public gardens, which were so near to Everything, and meditated with annoyance on the stupidity, the obstinacy, and heartlessness of women.

"She is not in the very least sorry for me," he thought of his sister-in-law. "She cannot even understand my sorrow. And what of her?" He was thinking of his daughter. "She knows what all this means to me—the torture. What a blow in one's old age! My days will be shortened by it! But I'd rather have it over than endure this agony. And all that 'pour les beaux yeux d'un chenapan'—oh!" he moaned; and a wave of hatred and fury arose in him as he thought of what would be said in the town when every one knew. (And no doubt every one knew already.) Such a feeling of rage possessed him that he would have liked to beat it into her head, and make her understand what she had done. These women never understand. "It is quite near Everything," suddenly came to his mind, and getting out his note-book, he found her address. Vera Ivanovna Silvestrova, Kukonskaya Street, Abromov's house. She was living under this name. He left the gardens and called a cab.

"Whom do you wish to see, sir?" asked the midwife, Maria Ivanovna, when he stepped on the narrow landing of the steep, stuffy staircase.

"Does Madame Silvestrova live here?"

"Vera Ivanovna? Yes; please come in. She has gone out; she's gone to the shop round the corner. But she'll be back in a minute."

Michael Ivanovich followed the stout figure of Maria Ivanovna into a tiny parlour, and from the next room came the screams of a baby, sounding cross and peevish, which filled him with disgust. They cut him like a knife.

Maria Ivanovna apologised, and went into the room, and he could hear her soothing the child. The child became quiet, and she returned.

"That is her baby; she'll be back in a minute. You are a friend of hers, I suppose?"

"Yes—a friend—but I think I had better come back later on," said Michael Ivanovich, preparing to go. It was too unbearable, this prepara-tion to meet her, and any explanation seemed impossible.

He had just turned to leave, when he heard quick, light steps on the stairs, and he recognised Lisa's voice.

"Maria Ivanovna—has he been crying while I've been gone—I was—"

Then she saw her father. The parcel she was carrying fell from her hands.

"Father!" she cried, and stopped in the doorway, white and trembling.

He remained motionless, staring at her. She had grown so thin. Her eyes were larger, her nose sharper, her hands worn and bony. He nei-ther knew what to do, nor what to say. He forgot all his grief about his dishonour. He only felt sorrow, infinite sorrow for her; sorrow for her thinness, and for her miserable rough clothing; and most of all, for her pitiful face and imploring eyes.

"Father—forgive," she said, moving towards him.

"Forgive—forgive me," he murmured; and he began to sob like a child, kissing her face and hands, and wetting them with his tears.

In his pity for her he understood himself. And when he saw himself as he was, he realised how he had wronged her, how guilty he had been in his pride, in his coldness, even in his anger towards her. He was glad that it was he who was guilty, and that he had nothing to forgive, but that he himself needed forgiveness. She took him to her tiny room, and told him how she lived; but she did not show him the child, nor did she mention the past, knowing how painful it would be to him.

He told her that she must live differently.

"Yes; if I could only live in the country," said she.

"We will talk it over," he said. Suddenly the child began to wail and to scream. She opened her eyes very wide; and, not taking them from her father's face, remained hesitating and motionless.

"Well—I suppose you must feed him," said Michael Ivanovich, and frowned with the obvious effort.

She got up, and suddenly the wild idea seized her to show him whom she loved so deeply the thing she now loved best of all in the world. But first she looked at her father's face. Would he be angry or not? His face revealed no anger, only suffering.

"Yes, go, go," said he; "God bless you. Yes. I'll come again to-morrow, and we will decide. Good-bye, my darling—good-bye." Again he found it hard to swallow the lump in his throat.

When Michael Ivanovich returned to his brother's house, Alexandra Dmitrievna immediately rushed to him.

"Well?"

"Well? Nothing."

"Have you seen?" she asked, guessing from his expression that something had happened.

"Yes," he answered shortly, and began to cry. "I'm getting old and stupid," said he, mastering his emotion.

"No; you are growing wise—very wise."

THERE ARE NO GUILTY PEOPLE

I

MINE is a strange and wonderful lot! The chances are that there is not a single wretched beggar suffering under the luxury and oppression of the rich who feels anything like as keenly as I do either the injustice, the cruelty, and the horror of their oppression of and contempt for the poor; or the grinding humiliation and misery which befall the great majority of the workers, the real producers of all that makes life possible. I have felt this for a long time, and as the years have passed by the feeling has grown and grown, until recently it reached its climax. Although I feel all this so vividly, I still live on amid the depravity and sins of rich society; and I cannot leave it, because I have neither the knowledge nor the strength to do so. I cannot. I do not know how to change my life so that my physical needs—food, sleep, clothing, my going to and fro—may be satisfied without a sense of shame and wrongdoing in the position which I fill.

There was a time when I tried to change my position, which was not in harmony with my conscience; but the conditions created by the past, by my family and its claims upon me, were so complicated that they would not let me out of their grasp, or rather, I did not know how to free myself. I had not the strength. Now that I am over eighty and have become feeble, I have given up trying to free myself; and, strange to say, as my feebleness increases I realise more and more strongly the wrongfulness of my position, and it grows more and more intolerable to me.

It has occurred to me that I do not occupy this position for nothing: that Providence intended that I should lay bare the truth of my feelings, so that I might atone for all that causes my suffering, and might perhaps open the eyes of those—or at least of some of those—who are still blind to what I see so clearly, and thus might lighten the burden of that vast majority who, under existing conditions, are subjected to bodily and spiritual suffering by those who deceive them and also deceive themselves. Indeed, it may be that the position which I occupy gives me special facilities for revealing the artificial and criminal relations which exist between men—for telling the whole truth in regard to that position without confusing the issue by attempting to vindicate myself, and without rousing the envy of the rich and feelings of oppression in the hearts of the poor and downtrodden. I am so placed that I not only have no desire to vindicate myself; but, on the contrary, I find it necessary to make an effort lest I should exaggerate the wickedness of the great among whom I live, of whose society I am ashamed, whose attitude towards their fellow-men I detest with my whole soul, though I find it impossible to separate my lot from theirs. But I must also avoid the error of those democrats and others who, in defending the oppressed and the enslaved, do not see their failings and mistakes, and who do not make sufficient allowance for the difficulties created, the mistakes inherited from the past, which in a degree lessens the responsibility of the upper classes.

Free from desire for self-vindication, free from fear of an emancipated people, free from that envy and hatred which the oppressed feel for their oppressors, I am in the best possible position to see the truth and to tell it. Perhaps that is why Providence placed me in such a position. I will do my best to turn it to account.

II

Alexander Ivanovich Volgin, a bachelor and a clerk in a Moscow bank at a salary of eight thousand roubles a year, a man much respected in his own set, was staying in a country-house. His host was a wealthy landowner, owning some twenty-five hundred acres, and had married his guest's cousin. Volgin, tired after an evening spent in playing vint[3] for small stakes with members of the family, went to his room and placed his watch, silver cigarette-case, pocket-book, big leather purse, and pocket-brush and comb on a small table covered with a white cloth, and then, taking off his coat, waistcoat, shirt, trousers, and underclothes, his silk socks and English boots, put on his nightshirt and dressing-gown. His watch pointed to midnight. Volgin smoked a cigarette, lay on his face for about five minutes reviewing the day's impressions; then, blowing out his candle, he turned over on his side and fell asleep about one

---

3   A game of cards similar to auction bridge.

o'clock, in spite of a good deal of restlessness. Awaking next morning at eight he put on his slippers and dressing-gown, and rang the bell.

The old butler, Stephen, the father of a family and the grandfather of six grandchildren, who had served in that house for thirty years, entered the room hurriedly, with bent legs, carrying in the newly blackened boots which Volgin had taken off the night before, a well-brushed suit, and a clean shirt. The guest thanked him, and then asked what the weather was like (the blinds were drawn so that the sun should not prevent any one from sleeping till eleven o'clock if he were so inclined), and whether his hosts had slept well. He glanced at his watch—it was still early—and began to wash and dress. His water was ready, and everything on the washing-stand and dressing-table was ready for use and properly laid out—his soap, his tooth and hair brushes, his nail scissors and files. He washed his hands and face in a leisurely fashion, cleaned and manicured his nails, pushed back the skin with the towel, and sponged his stout white body from head to foot. Then he began to brush his hair. Standing in front of the mirror, he first brushed his curly beard, which was beginning to turn grey, with two English brushes, parting it down the middle. Then he combed his hair, which was already showing signs of getting thin, with a large tortoise-shell comb. Putting on his underlinen, his socks, his boots, his trousers—which were held up by elegant braces—and his waistcoat, he sat down coatless in an easy chair to rest after dressing, lit a cigarette, and began to think where he should go for a walk that morning—to the park or to Littleports (what a funny name for a wood!). He thought he would go to Littleports. Then he must answer Simon Nicholaevich's letter; but there was time enough for that. Getting up with an air of resolution, he took out his watch. It was already five minutes to nine. He put his watch into his waistcoat pocket, and his purse—with all that was left of the hundred and eighty roubles he had taken for his journey, and for the incidental expenses of his fortnight's stay with his cousin—and then he placed into his trouser pocket his cigarette-case and electric cigarette-lighter, and two clean handkerchiefs into his coat pockets, and went out of the room, leaving as usual the mess and confusion which he had made to be cleared up by Stephen, an old man of over fifty. Stephen expected Volgin to "remunerate" him, as he said, being so accustomed to the work that he did not feel the slightest repugnance for it. Glancing at a mirror, and feeling satisfied with his appearance, Volgin went into the dining-room.

There, thanks to the efforts of the housekeeper, the footman, and under-butler—the latter had risen at dawn in order to run home to sharpen his son's scythe—breakfast was ready. On a spotless white cloth stood a boiling, shiny, silver samovar (at least it looked like silver), a coffee-pot, hot milk, cream, butter, and all sorts of fancy white bread and biscuits. The only persons at table were the second son of the house, his tutor (a student), and the secretary. The host, who was an active member of the Zemstvo and a great farmer, had already left the house, having gone at eight o'clock to attend to his work. Volgin, while drinking his coffee, talked to the student and the secretary about the weather, and yesterday's vint, and discussed Theodorite's peculiar behaviour the night before, as he had been very rude to his father without the slightest cause. Theodorite was the grown-up son of the house, and a ne'er-do-well. His name was Theodore, but some one had once called him Theodorite either as a joke or to tease him; and, as it seemed funny, the name stuck to him, although his doings were no longer in the least amusing. So it was now. He had been to the university, but left it in his second year, and joined a regiment of horse guards; but he gave that up also, and was now living in the country, doing nothing, finding fault, and feeling discontented with everything. Theodorite was still in bed: so were the other members of the household—Anna Mikhailovna, its mistress; her sister, the widow of a general; and a landscape painter who lived with the family.

Volgin took his panama hat from the hall table (it had cost twenty roubles) and his cane with its carved ivory handle, and went out. Crossing the veranda, gay with flowers, he walked through the flower garden, in the centre of which was a raised round bed, with rings of red, white, and blue flowers, and the initials of the mistress of the house done in carpet bedding in the centre. Leaving the flower garden Volgin entered the avenue of lime trees, hundreds of years old, which peasant girls were tidying and sweeping with spades and brooms. The gardener was busy measuring, and a boy was bringing something in a cart. Passing these Volgin went into the park of at least a hundred and twenty-five acres, filled with fine old trees, and intersected by a network of well-kept walks. Smoking as he strolled Volgin took his favourite path past the summer-house into the fields beyond. It was pleasant in the park, but it was still nicer in the fields. On the right some women who were digging potatoes formed a mass of bright red and white colour; on the left were wheat fields, meadows, and grazing cattle; and in the foreground, slightly to the right, were the dark, dark oaks of Littleports. Volgin took a deep breath, and felt glad that he was alive, especially here in his cousin's home, where he was so thoroughly enjoying the rest from his work at the bank.

"Lucky people to live in the country," he thought. "True, what with his farming and his Zemstvo, the owner of the estate has very little peace even in the country, but that is his own lookout." Volgin shook his head, lit another cigarette, and, stepping out firmly with his powerful feet clad in his thick English boots, began to think of the heavy winter's work in the bank that was in front of him. "I shall be there every day from ten to two, sometimes even till five. And the board meetings . . . And private interviews with clients. . . . Then the Duma. Whereas here. . . . It is delightful. It may be a little dull, but it is not for long." He smiled. After a stroll in Littleports he turned back, going straight across a fallow field which was being ploughed. A herd of cows, calves, sheep, and pigs, which belonged to the village community, was grazing there. The shortest way to the park was to pass through the herd. He frightened the sheep, which ran away one after another, and were followed by the pigs, of which two little ones stared solemnly at him. The shepherd boy called to the sheep and cracked his whip. "How far behind Europe we are," thought Volgin, recalling his frequent holidays abroad. "You would not find a single cow like that anywhere in Europe." Then, wanting to find out where the path which branched off from the one he was on led to and who was the owner of the herd, he called to the boy.

"Whose herd is it?"

The boy was so filled with wonder, verging on terror, when he gazed at the hat, the well-brushed beard, and above all the gold-rimmed eyeglasses, that he could not reply at once. When Volgin repeated his question the boy pulled himself together, and said, "Ours." "But whose is 'ours'?" said Volgin, shaking his head and smiling. The boy was wearing shoes of plaited birch bark, bands of linen round his legs, a dirty, unbleached shirt ragged at the shoulder, and a cap the peak of which had been torn.

"Whose is 'ours'?"

"The Pirogov village herd."

"How old are you?

"I don't know."

"Can you read?"

"No, I can't."

"Didn't you go to school?"

"Yes, I did."

"Couldn't you learn to read?"

"No."

"Where does that path lead?"

The boy told him, and Volgin went on towards the house, thinking how he would chaff Nicholas Petrovich about the deplorable condition of the village schools in spite of all his efforts.

On approaching the house Volgin looked at his watch, and saw that it was already past eleven. He remembered that Nicholas Petrovich was going to drive to the nearest town, and that he had meant to give him a letter to post to Moscow; but the letter was not written. The letter was a very important one to a friend, asking him to bid for him for a picture of the Madonna which was to be offered for sale at an auction. As he reached the house he saw at the door four big, well-fed, well-groomed, thoroughbred horses harnessed to a carriage, the black lacquer of which glistened in the sun. The coachman was seated on the box in a kaftan, with a silver belt, and the horses were jingling their silver bells from time to time.

A bare-headed, barefooted peasant in a ragged kaftan stood at the front door. He bowed. Volgin asked what he wanted.

"I have come to see Nicholas Petrovich."

"What about?"

"Because I am in distress—my horse has died."

Volgin began to question him. The peasant told him how he was situated. He had five children, and this had been his only horse. Now it was gone. He wept.

"What are you going to do?"

"To beg." And he knelt down, and remained kneeling in spite of Volgin's expostulations.

"What is your name?"

"Mitri Sudarikov," answered the peasant, still kneeling.

Volgin took three roubles from his purse and gave them to the peasant, who showed his gratitude by touching the ground with his forehead, and then went into the house. His host was standing in the hall.

"Where is your letter?" he asked, approaching Volgin; "I am just off."

"I'm awfully sorry, I'll write it this minute, if you will let me. I forgot all about it. It's so pleasant here that one can forget anything."

"All right, but do be quick. The horses have already been standing a quarter of an hour, and the flies are biting viciously. Can you wait, Arsenty?" he asked the coachman.

"Why not?" said the coachman, thinking to himself, "why do they order the horses when they aren't ready? The rush the grooms and I had—just to stand here and feed the flies."

"Directly, directly," Volgin went towards his room, but turned back to ask Nicholas Petrovich about the begging peasant.

"Did you see him?—He's a drunkard, but still he is to be pitied. Do be quick!"

Volgin got out his case, with all the requisites for writing, wrote the letter, made out a cheque for a hundred and eighty roubles, and, sealing down the envelope, took it to Nicholas Petrovich.

"Good-bye."

Volgin read the newspapers till luncheon. He only read the Liberal papers: The Russian Gazette, Speech, sometimes The Russian Word—but he would not touch The New Times, to which his host subscribed.

While he was scanning at his ease the political news, the Tsar's doings, the doings of President, and ministers and decisions in the Duma, and was just about to pass on to the general news, theatres, science, murders and cholera, he heard the luncheon bell ring.

Thanks to the efforts of upwards of ten human beings—counting laundresses, gardeners, cooks, kitchen-maids, butlers and footmen—the table was sumptuously laid for eight, with silver waterjugs, decanters, kvass, wine, mineral waters, cut glass, and fine table linen, while two men-servants were continually hurrying to and fro, bringing in and serving, and then clearing away the hors d'oeuvre and the various hot and cold courses.

The hostess talked incessantly about everything that she had been doing, thinking, and saying; and she evidently considered that everything that she thought, said, or did was perfect, and that it would please every one except those who were fools. Volgin felt and knew that everything she said was stupid, but it would never do to let it be seen, and so he kept up the conversation. Theodorite was glum and silent; the student occasionally exchanged a few words with the widow. Now and again there was a pause in the conversation, and then Theodorite interposed, and every one became miserably depressed. At such moments the hostess ordered some dish that had not been served, and the footman hurried off to the kitchen, or to the housekeeper, and hurried back again. Nobody felt inclined either to talk or to eat. But they all forced themselves to eat and to talk, and so luncheon went on.

The peasant who had been begging because his horse had died was named Mitri Sudarikov. He had spent the whole day before he went to the squire over his dead horse. First of all he went to the knacker, Sanin, who lived in a village near. The knacker was out, but he waited for him, and it was dinner-time when he had finished bargaining over the price of the skin. Then he borrowed a neighbour's horse to take his own to a field to be buried, as it is forbidden to bury dead animals near a village. Adrian would not lend his horse because he was getting in his potatoes, but Stephen took pity on Mitri and gave way to his persuasion. He even lent a hand in lifting the dead horse into the cart. Mitri tore off the shoes from the forelegs and gave them to his wife. One was broken, but the other one was whole. While he was digging the grave with a spade which was very blunt, the knacker appeared and took off the skin; and the carcass was then thrown into the hole and covered up. Mitri felt tired, and went into Matrena's hut, where he drank half a bottle of vodka with Sanin to console himself. Then he went home, quarrelled with his wife, and lay down to sleep on the hay. He did not undress, but slept just as he was, with a ragged coat for a coverlet. His wife was in the hut with the girls—there were four of them, and the youngest was only five weeks old. Mitri woke up before dawn as usual. He groaned as the memory of the day before broke in upon him—how the horse had struggled and struggled, and then fallen down. Now there was no horse, and all he had was the price of the skin, four roubles and eighty kopeks. Getting up he arranged the linen bands on his legs, and went through the yard into the hut. His wife was putting straw into the stove with one hand, with the other she was holding a baby girl to her breast, which was hanging out of her dirty chemise.

Mitri crossed himself three times, turning towards the corner in which the ikons hung, and repeated some utterly meaningless words, which he called prayers, to the Trinity and the Virgin, the Creed and our Father.

"Isn't there any water?"

"The girl's gone for it. I've got some tea. Will you go up to the squire?"

"Yes, I'd better." The smoke from the stove made him cough. He took a rag off the wooden bench and went into the porch. The girl had just come back with the water. Mitri filled his mouth with water from the pail and squirted it out on his hands, took some more in his mouth to wash his face, dried himself with the rag, then parted and smoothed his curly hair with his fingers and went out. A little girl of about ten, with nothing on but a dirty shirt, came towards him. "Good-morning, Uncle Mitri," she said; "you are to come and thrash." "All right, I'll come," replied Mitri. He understood that he was expected to return the help given the week before by Kumushkir, a man as poor as he was himself, when he was thrashing his own corn with a horse-driven machine.

"Tell them I'll come—I'll come at lunch time. I've got to go to Ugrumi." Mitri went back to the hut, and changing his birch-bark shoes and the linen bands on his legs, started off to see the squire. After he had got three roubles from Volgin, and the same sum from Nicholas Petrovich, he returned to his house, gave the money to his wife, and went to his neighbour's. The thrashing machine was humming, and the driver was shouting. The lean horses were going slowly round him, straining at their traces. The driver was shouting to them in a monotone, "Now, there, my dears." Some women were unbinding sheaves, others were raking up the scattered straw and ears, and others again were gathering great armfuls of corn and handing them to the men to feed the machine. The work was in full swing. In the kitchen garden, which Mitri had to pass, a girl, clad only in a long shirt, was digging potatoes which she put into a basket.

"Where's your grandfather?" asked Mitri. "He's in the barn." Mitri went to the barn and set to work at once. The old man of eighty knew of Mitri's trouble. After greeting him, he gave him his place to feed the machine.

Mitri took off his ragged coat, laid it out of the way near the fence, and then began to work vigorously, raking the corn together and throwing it into the machine. The work went on without interruption until the dinner-hour. The cocks had crowed two or three times, but no one paid any attention to them; not because the workers did not believe them, but because they were scarcely heard for the noise of the work and the talk about it. At last the whistle of the squire's steam thrasher sounded three miles away, and then the owner came into the barn. He was a straight old man of eighty. "It's time to stop," he said; "it's dinner-time." Those at work seemed to redouble their efforts. In a moment the straw was cleared away; the grain that had been thrashed was separated from the chaff and brought in, and then the workers went into the hut.

The hut was smoke-begrimed, as its stove had no chimney, but it had been tidied up, and benches stood round the table, making room for all those who had been working, of whom there were nine, not counting the owners. Bread, soup, boiled potatoes, and kvass were placed on the table.

An old one-armed beggar, with a bag slung over his shoulder, came in with a crutch during the meal.

"Peace be to this house. A good appetite to you. For Christ's sake give me something."

"God will give it to you," said the mistress, already an old woman, and the daughter-in-law of the master. "Don't be angry with us." An old man, who was still standing near the door, said, "Give him some bread, Martha. How can you?"

"I am only wondering whether we shall have enough." "Oh, it is wrong, Martha. God tells us to help the poor. Cut him a slice."

Martha obeyed. The beggar went away. The man in charge of the thrashing-machine got up, said grace, thanked his hosts, and went away to rest.

Mitri did not lie down, but ran to the shop to buy some tobacco. He was longing for a smoke. While he smoked he chatted to a man from Demensk, asking the price of cattle, as he saw that he would not be able to manage without selling a cow. When he returned to the others, they were already back at work again; and so it went on till the evening.

Among these downtrodden, duped, and defrauded men, who are becoming demoralised by overwork, and being gradually done to death by underfeeding, there are men living who consider themselves Christians; and others so enlightened that they feel no further need for Christianity or for any religion, so superior do they appear in their own esteem. And yet their hideous, lazy lives are supported by the degrading, excessive labour of these slaves, not to mention the labour of millions of other slaves, toiling in factories to produce samovars, silver, carriages, machines, and the like for their use. They live among these horrors, seeing them and yet not seeing them, although often kind at heart—old men and women, young men and maidens, mothers and children—poor children who are being vitiated and trained into moral blindness.

Here is a bachelor grown old, the owner of thousands of acres, who has lived a life of idleness, greed, and over-indulgence, who reads The New Times, and is astonished that the government can be so unwise as to permit Jews to enter the university. There is his guest, formerly the governor of a province, now a senator with a big salary, who reads with satisfaction that a congress of lawyers has passed a resolution in favor of capital punishment. Their political enemy, N. P., reads a liberal paper, and cannot understand the blindness of the government in allowing the union of Russian men to exist.

Here is a kind, gentle mother of a little girl reading a story to her about Fox, a dog that lamed some rabbits. And here is this little girl. During her walks she sees other children, barefooted, hungry, hunting for green apples that have fallen from the trees; and, so accustomed is she to the sight, that these children do not seem to her to be children such as she is, but only part of the usual surroundings—the familiar landscape.

Why is this?

THE YOUNG TSAR

THE young Tsar had just ascended the throne. For five weeks he had worked without ceasing, in the way that Tsars are accustomed to work. He had been attending to reports, signing papers, receiving ambassadors and high officials who came to be presented to him, and reviewing troops. He was tired, and as a traveller exhausted by heat and thirst longs for a draught of water and for rest, so he longed for a respite of just one day at least from receptions, from speeches, from parades—a few free hours to spend like an ordinary human being with his young, clever, and beautiful wife, to whom he had been married only a month before.

It was Christmas Eve. The young Tsar had arranged to have a complete rest that evening. The night before he had worked till very late at documents which his ministers of state had left for him to examine. In the morning he was present at the Te Deum, and then at a military service. In the afternoon he received official visitors; and later he had been obliged to listen to the reports of three ministers of state, and had given his assent to many important matters. In his conference with the Minister of Finance he had agreed to an increase of duties on imported goods, which should in the future add many millions to the State revenues. Then he sanctioned the sale of brandy by the Crown in various parts of the country, and signed a decree permitting the sale of alcohol in villages having markets. This was also calculated to increase the principal revenue to the State, which was derived from the sale of spirits. He had also approved of the issuing of a new gold loan required for a financial negotiation. The Minister of justice having reported on the complicated case of the succession of the Baron Snyders, the young Tsar confirmed the decision by his signature; and also approved the new rules relating to the application of Article 1830 of the penal code, providing for the punishment of tramps. In his conference with the Minister of the Interior he ratified the order concerning the collection of taxes in arrears, signed the order settling what measures should be taken in regard to the persecution of religious dissenters, and also one providing for the continuance of martial law in those provinces where it had already been established. With the Minister of War he arranged for the nomination of a new Corps Commander for the raising of recruits, and for punishment of breach of discipline. These things kept him occupied till dinner-time, and even then his freedom was not complete. A number of high officials had been invited to dinner, and he was obliged to talk to them: not in the way he felt disposed to do, but according to what he was expected to say. At last the tiresome dinner was over, and the guests departed.

The young Tsar heaved a sigh of relief, stretched himself and retired to his apartments to take off his uniform with the decorations on it, and to don the jacket he used to wear before his accession to the throne. His young wife had also retired to take off her dinner-dress, remarking that she would join him presently.

When he had passed the row of footmen who were standing erect before him, and reached his room; when he had thrown off his heavy uniform and put on his jacket, the young Tsar felt glad to be free from work; and his heart was filled with a tender emotion which sprang from the consciousness of his freedom, of his joyous, robust young life, and of his love. He threw himself on the sofa, stretched out his legs upon it, leaned his head on his hand, fixed his gaze on the dull glass shade of the lamp, and then a sensation which he had not experienced since his childhood,—the pleasure of going to sleep, and a drowsiness that was irresistible—suddenly came over him.

"My wife will be here presently and will find me asleep. No, I must not go to sleep," he thought. He let his elbow drop down, laid his cheek in the palm of his hand, made himself comfortable, and was so utterly happy that he only felt a desire not to be aroused from this delightful state.

And then what happens to all of us every day happened to him—he fell asleep without knowing himself when or how. He passed from one state into another without his will having any share in it, without even desiring it, and without regretting the state out of which he had passed. He fell into a heavy sleep which was like death. How long he had slept he did not know, but he was suddenly aroused by the soft touch of a hand upon his shoulder.

"It is my darling, it is she," he thought. "What a shame to have dozed off!"

But it was not she. Before his eyes, which were wide open and blinking at the light, she, that charming and beautiful creature whom he was expecting, did not stand, but *he* stood. Who *he* was the young Tsar did not know, but somehow it did not strike him that he was a stranger whom he had never seen before. It seemed as if he had known him for a long time and was fond of him, and as if he trusted him as he would trust himself. He had expected his beloved wife, but in her stead that man whom he had never seen before had come. Yet to the young Tsar, who was far from feeling regret or astonishment, it seemed not only a most natural, but also a necessary thing to happen.

"Come!" said the stranger.

"Yes, let us go," said the young Tsar, not knowing where he was to go, but quite aware that he could not help submitting to the command of the stranger. "But how shall we go?" he asked.

"In this way."

The stranger laid his hand on the Tsar's head, and the Tsar for a moment lost consciousness. He could not tell whether he had been unconscious a long or a short time, but when he recovered his senses he found himself in a strange place. The first thing he was aware of was a strong and stifling smell of sewage. The place in which he stood was a broad passage lit by the red glow of two dim lamps. Running along one side of the passage was a thick wall with windows protected by iron gratings. On the other side were doors secured with locks. In the passage stood a soldier, leaning up against the wall, asleep. Through the doors the young Tsar heard the muffled sound of living human beings: not of one alone, but of many. *he* was standing at the side of the young Tsar, and pressing his shoulder slightly with his soft hand, pushed him to the first door, unmindful of the sentry. The young Tsar felt he could not do otherwise than yield, and approached the door. To his amazement the sentry looked straight at him, evidently without seeing him, as he neither straightened himself up nor saluted, but yawned loudly and, lifting his hand, scratched the back of his neck. The door had a small hole, and in obedience to the pressure of the hand that pushed him, the young Tsar approached a step nearer and put his eye to the small opening. Close to the door, the foul smell that stifled him was stronger, and the young Tsar hesitated to go nearer, but the hand pushed him on. He leaned forward, put his eye close to the opening, and suddenly ceased to perceive the odour. The sight he saw deadened his sense of smell. In a large room, about ten yards long and six yards wide, there walked unceasingly from one end to the other, six men in long grey coats, some in felt boots, some barefoot. There were over twenty men in all in the room, but in that first moment the young Tsar only saw those who were walking with quick, even, silent steps. It was a horrid sight to watch the continual, quick, aimless movements of the men who passed and overtook each other, turning sharply when they reached the wall, never looking at one another, and evidently concentrated each on his own thoughts. The young Tsar had observed a similar sight one day when he was watching a tiger in a menagerie pacing rapidly with noiseless tread from one end of his cage to the other, waving its tail, silently turning when it reached the bars, and looking at nobody. Of these men one, apparently a young peasant, with curly hair, would have been hand-some were it not for the unnatural pallor of his face, and the concen-trated, wicked, scarcely human, look in his eyes. Another was a Jew, hairy and gloomy. The third was a lean old man, bald, with a beard that had been shaven and had since grown like bristles. The fourth was extraordinarily heavily built, with well-developed muscles, a low receding forehead and a flat nose. The fifth was hardly more than a boy, long, thin, obviously consumptive. The sixth was small and dark, with nervous, convulsive movements. He walked as if he were skipping, and muttered continuously to himself. They were all walk-ing rapidly backwards and forwards past the hole through which the young Tsar was looking. He watched their faces and their gait with keen interest. Having examined them closely, he presently became aware of a number of other men at the back of the room, standing round, or lying on the shelf that served as a bed. Standing close to the door he also saw the pail which caused such an unbearable stench. On the shelf about ten men, entirely covered with their cloaks, were sleeping. A red-haired man with a huge beard was sitting sideways on the shelf, with his shirt off. He was examining it, lifting it up to the light, and evidently catching the vermin on it. Another man, aged and white as snow, stood with his profile turned towards the door. He was praying, crossing himself, and bowing low, apparently so ab-sorbed in his devotions as to be oblivious of all around him.

"I see—this is a prison," thought the young Tsar. "They certainly deserve pity. It is a dreadful life. But it cannot be helped. It is their own fault."

But this thought had hardly come into his head before *he*, who was his guide, replied to it.

"They are all here under lock and key by your order. They have all been sentenced in your name. But far from meriting their present condition which is due to your human judgment, the greater part of them are far better than you or those who were their judges and who keep them here. This one"—he pointed to the handsome, curly-headed fellow—"is a murderer. I do not consider him more guilty than those who kill in war or in duelling, and are rewarded for their deeds. He had neither education nor moral guidance, and his life had been cast among thieves and drunkards. This lessens his guilt, but he has done wrong, nevertheless, in being a murderer. He killed a merchant, to rob him. The other man, the Jew, is a thief, one of a gang of thieves. That uncommonly strong fellow is a horse-stealer, and guilty also, but compared with others not as culpable. Look!"—and suddenly the young Tsar found himself in an open field on a vast frontier. On the right were potato fields; the plants had been rooted out, and were lying in heaps, blackened by the frost; in alternate streaks were rows of winter corn. In the distance a little village with its tiled roofs was visible; on the left were fields of winter corn, and fields of stubble. No one was to be seen on any side, save a black human figure in front at the border-line, a gun slung on his back, and at his feet a dog. On the spot where the young Tsar stood, sitting beside him, almost at his feet, was a young Russian soldier with a green band on his cap, and with his rifle slung over his shoulders, who was rolling up a paper to make a cigarette. The soldier was obviously unaware of the presence of the young Tsar and his companion, and had not heard them. He did now turn round when the Tsar, who was standing directly over the soldier, asked, "Where are we?" "On the Prussian frontier," his guide answered. Suddenly, far away in front of them, a shot was fired. The soldier jumped to his feet, and seeing two men running, bent low to the ground, hastily put his tobacco into his pocket, and ran after one of them. "Stop, or I'll shoot!" cried the soldier. The fugitive, without stopping, turned his head and called out something evidently abusive or blasphemous.

"Damn you!" shouted the soldier, who put one foot a little forward and stopped, after which, bending his head over his rifle, and raising his right hand, he rapidly adjusted something, took aim, and, pointing the gun in the direction of the fugitive, probably fired, although no sound was heard. "Smokeless powder, no doubt," thought the young

Tsar, and looking after the fleeing man saw him take a few hurried steps, and bending lower and lower, fall to the ground and crawl on his hands and knees. At last he remained lying and did not move. The other fugitive, who was ahead of him, turned round and ran back to the man who was lying on the ground. He did something for him and then resumed his flight.

"What does all this mean?" asked the Tsar.

"These are the guards on the frontier, enforcing the revenue laws. That man was killed to protect the revenues of the State."

"Has he actually been killed?"

The guide again laid his hand upon the head of the young Tsar, and again the Tsar lost consciousness. When he had recovered his senses he found himself in a small room—the customs office. The dead body of a man, with a thin grizzled beard, an aquiline nose, and big eyes with the eyelids closed, was lying on the floor. His arms were thrown asunder, his feet bare, and his thick, dirty toes were turned up at right angles and stuck out straight. He had a wound in his side, and on his ragged cloth jacket, as well as on his blue shirt, were stains of clotted blood, which had turned black save for a few red spots here and there. A woman stood close to the wall, so wrapped up in shawls that her face could scarcely be seen. Motionless she gazed at the aquiline nose, the upturned feet, and the protruding eyeballs; sobbing and sighing, and drying her tears at long, regular intervals. A pretty girl of thirteen was standing at her mother's side, with her eyes and mouth wide open. A boy of eight clung to his mother's skirt, and looked intensely at his dead father without blinking.

From a door near them an official, an officer, a doctor, and a clerk with documents, entered. After them came a soldier, the one who had shot the man. He stepped briskly along behind his superiors, but the instant he saw the corpse he went suddenly pale, and quivered; and dropping his head stood still. When the official asked him whether that was the man who was escaping across the frontier, and at whom he had fired, he was unable to answer. His lips trembled, and his face twitched. "The s—s—s—" he began, but could not get out the words which he wanted to say. "The same, your excellency." The officials looked at each other and wrote something down.

"You see the beneficial results of that same system!"

In a room of sumptuous vulgarity two men sat drinking wine. One of them was old and grey, the other a young Jew. The young Jew was holding a roll of bank-notes in his hand, and was bargaining with the old man. He was buying smuggled goods.

"You've got 'em cheap," he said, smiling.

"Yes—but the risk—"

"This is indeed terrible," said the young Tsar; "but it cannot be avoided. Such proceedings are necessary."

His companion made no response, saying merely, "Let us move on," and laid his hand again on the head of the Tsar. When the Tsar recovered consciousness, he was standing in a small room lit by a shaded lamp. A woman was sitting at the table sewing. A boy of eight was bending over the table, drawing, with his feet doubled up under him in the armchair. A student was reading aloud. The father and daughter of the family entered the room noisily.

"You signed the order concerning the sale of spirits," said the guide to the Tsar.

"Well?" said the woman.

"He's not likely to live."

"What's the matter with him?"

"They've kept him drunk all the time."

"It's not possible!" exclaimed the wife.

"It's true. And the boy's only nine years old, that Vania Moroshkine."

"What did you do to try to save him?" asked the wife.

"I tried everything that could be done. I gave him an emetic and put a mustard-plaster on him. He has every symptom of delirium tremens."

"It's no wonder—the whole family are drunkards. Annisia is only a little better than the rest, and even she is generally more or less drunk," said the daughter.

"And what about your temperance society?" the student asked his sister.

"What can we do when they are given every opportunity of drinking? Father tried to have the public-house shut up, but the law is against him. And, besides, when I was trying to convince Vasily Ermiline that it was disgraceful to keep a public-house and ruin the people with drink, he answered very haughtily, and indeed got the better of me before the crowd: 'But I have a license with the Imperial eagle on it. If there was anything wrong in my business, the Tsar wouldn't have issued a decree authorising it.' Isn't it terrible? The whole village has been drunk for the last three days. And as for feast-days, it is simply horrible to think of! It has been proved conclusively that alcohol does no good in any case, but invariably does harm, and it has been demonstrated to be an absolute poison. Then, ninety-nine per cent. of the crimes in the world are committed through its influence. We all know how the standard of morality and the general welfare improved at once in all the countries where drinking has been suppressed—like Sweden and Finland, and we know that it can be suppressed by exercising a moral influence over the masses. But in our country the class which could exert that influence—the Government, the Tsar and his officials—simply encourage drink. Their main revenues are drawn from the continual drunkenness of the people. They drink themselves—they are always drinking the health of somebody: 'Gentlemen, the Regiment!' The preachers drink, the bishops drink—"

Again the guide touched the head of the young Tsar, who again lost consciousness. This time he found himself in a peasant's cottage. The peasant—a man of forty, with red face and blood-shot eyes—was furiously striking the face of an old man, who tried in vain to protect himself from the blows. The younger peasant seized the beard of the old man and held it fast.

"For shame! To strike your father—!"

"I don't care, I'll kill him! Let them send me to Siberia, I don't care!"

The women were screaming. Drunken officials rushed into the cottage and separated father and son. The father had an arm broken and the son's beard was torn out. In the doorway a drunken girl was making violent love to an old besotted peasant.

"They are beasts!" said the young Tsar.

Another touch of his guide's hand and the young Tsar awoke in a new place. It was the office of the justice of the peace. A fat, bald-headed man, with a double chin and a chain round his neck, had just risen from his seat, and was reading the sentence in a loud voice, while a crowd of peasants stood behind the grating. There was a woman in rags in the crowd who did not rise. The guard gave her a push.

"Asleep! I tell you to stand up!" The woman rose.

"According to the decree of his Imperial Majesty—" the judge began reading the sentence. The case concerned that very woman. She had taken away half a bundle of oats as she was passing the thrashing-floor of a landowner. The justice of the peace sentenced her to two months' imprisonment. The landowner whose oats had been stolen was among the audience. When the judge adjourned the court the landowner approached, and shook hands, and the judge entered into conversation with him. The next case was about a stolen samovar. Then there was a trial about some timber which had been cut, to the detriment of the landowner. Some peasants were being tried for having assaulted the constable of the district.

When the young Tsar again lost consciousness, he awoke to find himself in the middle of a village, where he saw hungry, half-frozen children and the wife of the man who had assaulted the constable broken down from overwork.

Then came a new scene. In Siberia, a tramp is being flogged with the lash, the direct result of an order issued by the Minister of justice. Again oblivion, and another scene. The family of a Jewish watchmaker is evicted for being too poor. The children are crying, and the Jew, Isaaks, is greatly distressed. At last they come to an arrangement, and he is allowed to stay on in the lodgings.

The chief of police takes a bribe. The governor of the province also secretly accepts a bribe. Taxes are being collected. In the village, while a cow is sold for payment, the police inspector is bribed by a factory owner, who thus escapes taxes altogether. And again a village court scene, and a sentence carried into execution—the lash!

"Ilia Vasilievich, could you not spare me that?"

"No."

The peasant burst into tears. "Well, of course, Christ suffered, and He bids us suffer too."

Then other scenes. The Stundists—a sect—being broken up and dispersed; the clergy refusing first to marry, then to bury a Protestant. Orders given concerning the passage of the Imperial railway train. Soldiers kept sitting in the mud—cold, hungry, and cursing. Decrees issued relating to the educational institutions of the Empress Mary Department. Corruption rampant in the foundling homes. An undeserved monument. Thieving among the clergy. The reinforcement of the political police. A woman being searched. A prison for convicts who are sentenced to be deported. A man being hanged for murdering a shop assistant.

Then the result of military discipline: soldiers wearing uniform and scoffing at it. A gipsy encampment. The son of a millionaire exempted from military duty, while the only support of a large family is forced to serve. The university: a teacher relieved of military service, while the most gifted musicians are compelled to perform it. Soldiers and their debauchery—and the spreading of disease.

Then a soldier who has made an attempt to desert. He is being tried. Another is on trial for striking an officer who has insulted his mother. He is put to death. Others, again, are tried for having re-fused to shoot. The runaway soldier sent to a disciplinary battalion and flogged to death. Another, who is guiltless, flogged, and his wounds sprinkled with salt till he dies. One of the superior officers stealing money belonging to the soldiers. Nothing but drunkenness, debauch-ery, gambling, and arrogance on the part of the authorities.

What is the general condition of the people: the children are half-starving and degenerate; the houses are full of vermin; an everlasting dull round of labour, of submission, and of sadness. On the other hand: ministers, governors of provinces, covetous, ambitious, full of vanity, and anxious to inspire fear.

"But where are men with human feelings?"

"I will show you where they are."

Here is the cell of a woman in solitary confinement at Schlussel-burg. She is going mad. Here is another woman—a girl—indisposed, violated by soldiers. A man in exile, alone, embittered, half-dead. A prison for convicts condemned to hard labour, and women flogged. They are many.

Tens of thousands of the best people. Some shut up in prisons, oth-ers ruined by false education, by the vain desire to bring them up as we wish. But not succeeding in this, whatever might have been is ruined as well, for it is made impossible. It is as if we were trying to make buck-wheat out of corn sprouts by splitting the ears. One may spoil the corn, but one could never change it to buckwheat. Thus all the youth of the world, the entire younger generation, is being ruined.

But woe to those who destroy one of these little ones, woe to you if you destroy even one of them. On your soul, however, are hosts of them, who have been ruined in your name, all of those over whom your power extends.

"But what can I do?" exclaimed the Tsar in despair. "I do not wish to torture, to flog, to corrupt, to kill any one! I only want the welfare of all. Just as I yearn for happiness myself, so I want the world to be happy as well. Am I actually responsible for everything that is done in my name? What can I do? What am I to do to rid myself of such a responsibility? What can I do? I do not admit that the responsibil-ity for all this is mine. If I felt myself responsible for one-hundredth part of it, I would shoot myself on the spot. It would not be possible to live if that were true. But how can I put an end, to all this evil? It is bound up with the very existence of the State. I am the head of the State! What am I to do? Kill myself? Or abdicate? But that would mean renouncing my duty. O God, O God, God, help me!" He burst into tears and awoke.

"How glad I am that it was only a dream," was his first thought. But when he began to recollect what he had seen in his dream, and to compare it with actuality, he realised that the problem propounded to him in dream remained just as important and as insoluble now that he was awake. For the first time the young Tsar became aware of the heavy responsibility weighing on him, and was aghast. His thoughts no longer turned to the young Queen and to the happiness he had anticipated for that evening, but became centred on the unanswerable question which hung over him: "What was to be done?"

In a state of great agitation he arose and went into the next room. An old courtier, a co-worker and friend of his father's, was standing there in the middle of the room in conversation with the young Queen, who was on her way to join her husband. The young Tsar approached them, and addressing his conversation principally to the old courtier, told him what he had seen in his dream and what doubts the dream had left in his mind.

"That is a noble idea. It proves the rare nobility of your spirit," said the old man. "But forgive me for speaking frankly—you are too kind to be an emperor, and you exaggerate your responsibility. In the first place, the state of things is not as you imagine it to be. The people are not poor. They are well-to-do. Those who are poor are poor through their own fault. Only the guilty are punished, and if an unavoidable mistake does sometimes occur, it is like a thunderbolt—an accident, or the will of God. You have but one responsibility: to fulfil your task courageously and to retain the power that is given to you. You wish the best for your people and God sees that. As for the errors which you have committed unwittingly, you can pray for forgiveness, and God will guide you and pardon you. All the more because you have done nothing that demands forgiveness, and there never have been and never will be men possessed of such extraordinary qualities as you and your father. Therefore all we implore you to do is to live, and to reward our endless devotion and love with your favour, and every one, save scoundrels who deserve no happiness, will be happy."

"What do you think about that?" the young Tsar asked his wife.

"I have a different opinion," said the clever young woman, who had been brought up in a free country. "I am glad you had that dream, and I agree with you that there are grave responsibilities resting upon you. I have often thought about it with great anxiety, and I think there is a simple means of casting off a part of the responsibility you are unable to bear, if not all of it. A large proportion of the power which is too heavy for you, you should delegate to the people, to its representatives, reserving for yourself only the supreme control, that is, the general direction of the affairs of State."

The Queen had hardly ceased to expound her views, when the old courtier began eagerly to refute her arguments, and they started a polite but very heated discussion.

For a time the young Tsar followed their arguments, but presently he ceased to be aware of what they said, listening only to the voice of him who had been his guide in the dream, and who was now speaking audibly in his heart.

"You are not only the Tsar," said the voice, "but more. You are a human being, who only yesterday came into this world, and will perchance to-morrow depart out of it. Apart from your duties as a Tsar, of which that old man is now speaking, you have more immediate duties not by any means to be disregarded; human duties, not the duties of a Tsar towards his subjects, which are only accidental, but an eternal duty, the duty of a man in his relation to God, the duty toward your own soul, which is to save it, and also, to serve God in establishing his kingdom on earth. You are not to be guarded in your actions either by what has been or what will be, but only by what it is your own duty to do."

He opened his eyes—his wife was awakening him. Which of the three courses the young Tsar chose, will be told in fifty years.

www.ingramcontent.com/pod-product-compliance
Lightning Source LLC
Chambersburg PA
CBHW020247150626
46552CB00020B/642